COOKiE JAR

SHORT STORIES

MEGAN HILLS

Cookie Jar
Published in Australia in 2023 by Megan Hills
Olio3 Pty Ltd, PO Box 22 Waratah NSW 2298 Australia
ABN 73 134 136 002

Information on use permissions and/or content details should be
addressed to:
hello@meganhillsbooks.com
Visit: meganhillsbooks.com

Cover design by Laura Duffy
Typesetting by Rack and Rune Publishing
© 2023 Megan Hills
ISBN 978-0-9946017-7-3 (ebook)

ISBN 978-0-9946017-8-0 (paperback)

CONTENTS

I dedicate this book to you. While our distraction-addled culture may shorten your attention span by the day, you remain open to stories that may lift you, change you, and connect you.
Thank you.

WHOLE & TORN

[Sprinkle Cookie]

The art of Jessica Adams is surprising. Gazing long-distance at her works, one might assume 'photography'. Closer up, one might think 'painting'. Leaning in, breaking the COVID-1.5 metre rule, you blink twice before registering. It's collage.

'Collage on a freakin' towering pedestal of artistic excellence,' one established art critic said to their dog, because no one else was listening.

'Not a whiff of scrapbooking,' a liker quipped on Instagram to 2,365 followers.

It was true Jess Adams' work comprised an extraordinary number of small bits of coloured paper cut and stuck in a way never seen before. Eyebrows lift involuntarily when seeing Jessica Adams herself. Her refined beauty, her long straight red hair, and her wheelchair. Not a big surprise. Just enough to cause a small brow bounce before shifting focus to something else. But on the night of her exhibition opening, there was some special attention firmly on the artist. The kind of male attention unwelcome by women. Particularly by those who can't run.

'Apparently, I'm letting down the disability sector by not creating an exhibition on being a paraplegic,' Jess said to Kelly as they sat in a park near St Kilda beach, looking over the water. Right here was Bunurong Country. Behind the women pulsed Melbourne's jumble of high rises, sandstone, and tramlines. Melbourne was often cited as "Australia's most European city". Not so much "Wurundjeri Woi Wurrung Country". A mouthful for English tongues.

'Which brand of arsehole came up with that bullshit?' Kelly replied while focusing her Canon EOS 80D on a nearby tree.

'Someone talking to my mum.' Jess crunched on a Twistie, her fingers dusted in sticky gold. Her hands still looked quite nice, she noted to herself, given they were rough from cutting and sticking tiny bits of paper, and from pushing herself around. She moved around in a manual wheelchair as a preference to electric. There were many reasons for this. Manuals are easy to fold into cars, require less maintenance, and won't run out of charge. They are also easier to navigate in small spaces and crowds. For Jess, there was also the matter of finances, something perpetually at the forefront of her mind, as it is with most artists. But that didn't stop her salivating over the Pride Jazzy Air 2.0. In eleven seconds, with the touch of a button, she could elevate to the same height as if she were standing. No more awkward moments of people wondering if they should talk from above, bend down or squat. And she could see art as others see it. 'One day,' she murmured to herself on a semi-regular basis. But the versed response to anyone who asks about her choice of chair is, 'This baby keeps me fit,' reinforcing her point by displaying her impressive arm muscles, albeit pale and a bit freckly. She's proud of her elegant but strong upper body, which doesn't look muscular until she flexes. Jess is also grateful that her strength enables collaging small bits of paper over long periods of time, significantly longer than most artists could, given the back pain wasn't kicking-in. The act of creating may have been her breadwinner, but it was also her medicine. While she worked, all anxiety and self-doubt dissipated. She was in, what some might call, a state of grace.

'Nice of your mum to pass on the toxic message,' Kelly replied, disappearing behind her camera. 'Paraplegic exhibition,' she added in disgust. Jess looked across at her friend's dark hands and curly mop of dark hair, taking the shot. God knows what Kelly was capturing, but it would be something interesting. Kelly called herself a coconut before others did. She grew up urban, but something Wurundjeri had passed down in her DNA or in her spirit or both. Kelly noticed things in nature that Jess or anyone else would miss. She noticed even more things during the COVID lockdowns when nature got to run riot. As Jess and Kelly 'walked' down the street (Kelly swaggered, Jess cruised), they could be chewing the fat on the pandemic, the price of petrol or the fact they were both closing in on forty and still single. But at the end of the street, Kelly could roll-call the insects she saw, the birds she heard, the smell of the plants. When it came to nature, Jess called Kelly's ability 'high-res recall'. The photos Kelly took were for other people, anyone who was willing to look at them. She didn't need them herself, as she already had the images inside her, plus their sound, their smell, their feel. Her photos were interesting. Perhaps not at first glance, but something in them made people double-take.

Kelly helped herself to a handful of Twisties from Jess' packet. She held one up to the light and said, 'Corn, rice and wheat pulverised into the shape of a tiny poo,' before throwing it and the rest into her mouth.

'Don't dis the Twistie,' Jess replied, tucking a strand of her long red hair behind her ear before sliding a couple into her mouth and closing her eyes while crunching on their cheesy deliciousness.

'Have to admit, I forgot how good they are.' Kelly wiped the yellow powder residue from her hands onto her jeans before picking up her camera again. 'The last time I had them I was maybe twelve, thirteen.'

'I *would* say the same,' Jess said, 'except for that exhibition opening last month. You weren't there. They had these canapes that looked like something out of a Parisian degustation restaurant. Delicious. But the star of the edible art that evening was a single black matt platter of Twisties, spaced out just so.'

'For the kids?' Kelly looked sideways.

'There were no kids. For irony, maybe. Cool nostalgia?' she said, throwing a few more in her mouth.

'Pretentious wankers.'

'I thought I'd have Twisties at my opening,' Jess said through the side of her mouth.

'Great idea,' Kelly replied, distracted by something in a tree. Jess then offered the rest to Kelly, which got her attention. Tipping the rest of the packet from above into her open mouth like a baby bird, she then crunched and frowned. 'So, why wasn't I there?'

'At the black platter opening? You had that thing on,' Jess said, wiping her yellowed fingers on a tissue. 'The Aboriginal bat mitzvah.'

'That's right. Kippahs and clapsticks.' Kelly grinned before taking a photo of a nearby bush.

Jess used snapshots from her phone to help guide her collage compositions. Her next exhibition, 'Watching', was to be held at Optica Gallery, a small contemporary art space on Acland Street, a short stroll from where they were sitting. All the subjects of Jess' new collages were watching something. A father and son at a football match, a young girl with a surfboard reading the ocean's movements from the shore, a family watching television, Kelly peering at nature through her camera. All photo subjects had her permission to use their image as a guide. One work, entitled '*TV*', was extra special to Jess. It was of a prison warder watching a prisoner watching television. She didn't work off a photo of this exact scene. Instead, she sketched it. This branching out into an imagined scene, a concept designed by her, was a forward step in her practice. The exhibition had fifteen artworks in total. Each one took an eternity to create, but she had COVID to thank for the extra time. A silver lining.

'So,' Kelly said, wiping her fingers on her jeans before taking up the camera again. 'What did you say back to your mum?'

'What do you mean?'

'You know what I mean.' She was still one-eyed, peering through her lens, but the tone said it all. 'When your mum passed on this message about how your exhibition should have a paraplegic focus. Which we both know was probably her idea, by the way. Not someone she was talking to.' Kelly paused. 'Look, if you wanted to choose to have that focus, then no one would do it better. But that's not the point, is it?'

'I didn't dignify it with a response,' Jess said, regretting bringing it up. Then Jess laughed. 'Maybe if I created an exhibition about being a paraplegic, I could get a grant. It could pay for the whole thing, the framing. Any sales would be a bonus. Like, to pay for rent and food. Crazy indulgences like that.'

'Those bloody framing bills...' Kelly chuckled. But there was an edge to the humour.

'Yes, those framing bills. Combined with the time it takes to create each work. It's crippling me,' she said. 'Financially.'

'You'll sell out,' Kelly said, getting up to walk a couple of paces, then crouch on the grass. 'Your last exhibition did. People have been clawing to see more of your work since then. In the flesh, of course. COVID has just increased the salivation.'

'Maybe. Or is relying on the exhibition selling out post-lockdown a long shot? Everyone is just managing to stagger out of their homes. If I don't sell out this exhibition, I'll have to move back in with Mum.'

Kelly lowered the camera. 'Is that what Satan said? I mean, your mother?' Jess said nothing. 'We talked about this. Here we have a perfect example of how to practice being assertive, right? Channel your inner raging redhead. Speak up, boundaries, all that stuff. Stand up for yourself.'

'Stand on my own two feet?' Jess laughed. 'Are you calling me a sitting duck?'

'Ha ha,' Kelly said with sarcasm, then couldn't help but grin. 'But seriously. You are already well and truly on your own two feet. You have your own place and a fan-bloody-tastic art practice that's been generating serious traction over the past three years, despite the pandemic. No, this is about being a little more assertive in how you talk about yourself. How you address those who don't see your talent for what it is, and don't see you for who you really are.'

'Okay,' she sighed. 'Thanks for the kick up the arse.'

'You're welcome.'

Jess preferred to pick her battles, but Kelly would say Jess weaves from conflict like a ticklish boxer with a full bladder. And Kelly knew her well enough and long enough to make a solid call on the matter. They first met at art school almost a decade ago, finding common ground by being the oldest students in the class. In the beginning, it was tempting to be disdainful of the younger students with so little life experience. But they soon learned that age and life experience matter little when it came to art. Art cares about truths so personal (but also well-crafted) that they can't help but resonate with other people. The paradox of what is most yours is also most everyone else's. In art, vulnerability is king. But artists also needed a thick skin to make it through the technical traumas of art creation, the consistent rejection from galleries, and the agony of filling out grant applications. They had to work with a 'magical thinking' mindset while also being a practical A-to-B project manager who submitted tax returns. They had to be living opposites. No wonder so many artists turn to hard drugs and Twisties.

When Jess' exhibition opening finally happened, everyone felt a little exposed. It was post-COVID lockdown number six, and visitors to the gallery were wondering whether to wear masks, no longer mandatory. Making your own decisions after being told what to do for so long was throwing people. Drinking was to be had, but there were no chairs. For months, they had been told you have to sit down to drink (finding a chair wasn't a problem for Jess). But that rule had changed, hadn't it? It was a warm early December evening, and people were thirsty. No one was sure how they would celebrate Christmas, but coming out to casual events like this one served as a light practice run.

Jess sensed the early gatherers were careful around her, possibly assuming that being in a wheelchair meant she was immunocompromised. They were wrong, as her paralysis was below the waist and her lungs were better than most. But Jess worried the sight of her wheelchair might drive COVID-considerate people out of the gallery, so she sat at the back in a corner and observed with her teeth clenched to control her usual opening night jitters.

Kelly appeared from the compact gallery kitchen nearby with two glasses of Sauvignon Blanc. Dutch courage for Jess. Celebration for Kelly, who had just heard the news. Imogen, Jess' mother, couldn't make the opening due to possibly having COVID symptoms. Kelly was beaming. Jess looked over, touched by the vision of Kelly's new purple dress, bought especially for the evening. Kelly never wears dresses. It fitted perfectly, but she still looked a little awkward in it, saved only by the motorbike boots.

Swigging her glass while surveying the room, Kelly's buoyant mood dropped. She noticed the tentativeness of those arriving. The ingrained duty of social distancing distracted from looking at the works. 'Jesus,' Kelly said as she strode back to the kitchen. 'The people OUT THERE need ALCOHOL, damn it,' she yelled into the waiting staff. 'Buyers need to FUCKING RELAX and enjoy the artwork. ALCOHOL. NOW.' Kelly grabbed a platter of hors d'oeuvres as it was being carried out. 'Did you not hear me? Triage, for God's sake! ALCOHOL, people! Hold BACK the food!'

The blonde-coiffed gallery director, Lauretta Mason, caught the end of Kelly's trenches speech. With eyes glowering, she strode towards the kitchen as fast as her tight pencil skirt and Aminah Abdul-Jillil two-inch heels would allow. Opening her hot pink lips but keeping her teeth clenched, she was about to launch a hiss-whisper. But Kelly intercepted with flared nostrils. 'You want to make sales tonight?' Lauretta's lips came together as she nodded nervously. 'Then get OUT THERE,' Kelly pointed out to the crowd filling up the woman's own place of business. 'And take a bottle with you. Top up every glass in the room.' Wide-eyed, Lauretta nodded again, took an open bottle of Yarra Valley sparkling, promptly u-turned and trotted back into the throng.

'You promised Twisties, and I get squeaky tofu,' Kelly growled as she bit into an hors d'oeuvres that tasted like a softened eraser doused in ginger and soy.

'Viral transmission risk means no bowls of nibbles, including nuts, olives and Twisties,' Jess replied. 'Gallery policy in line with government recommendations. For this week anyway.'

'Explains why the other gallery spaced out the Twisties on the platters.' Kelly shrugged. 'We should have done spaced-out Twisties on enormous platters. Lots of them.'

'Black platters?'

'Black platters,' Kelly nodded.

'Next time,' she said. Opening night butterflies combined with her hatred of crowded rooms jangled her nerves. And, of course, there was the obvious problem. As always, she dreaded making other people feel uncomfortable by the mere sight of her wheelchair. Uncomfortable people made her feel uncomfortable.

'You look great,' Kelly said, already knowing what Jess was thinking. They had discussed many times what they termed 'freak factor funk', which happened mostly before Jess' exhibition openings. 'You're rocking that green dress. But if you had a miniature conjoined twin making weird noises, I might not be standing here.'

Jess took another sip of her wine. The nebulous contemporary sounds fed through hidden speakers, initially bouncing off the white walls and polished concrete floor, now softened by the increased number of bodies and drowned by voices. As the attendance number count increased, so did the room temperature. It was Wednesday night. A school night, but guests began partaking the complimentary wine, now flowing like New Zealand rapids due to Kelly's efforts. They drank like it was urgent medicine. In a way, it was. Jess surveyed the room. Some dressed as if attending the opera in Paris, others looked fresh from a construction site. There was no dress etiquette for exhibition openings anymore, and that pleased Jess. Choose your own adventure.

She watched those who were looking at her work, wondering what they were bringing to it. Most people didn't understand this. Art requires you to meet it halfway, to bring something of your own to the table. It's not like seeing a band with everyone moving to the same beat. The musicians, the crowd, the music, all one collective pulse. Bodies may have been close together in the gallery, but there were a multitude of quiet, personal responses going on out there. Or, at least, Jess hoped there were.

Those making their way to the back section of the room glanced across at her. Some would have known she was the artist, but some would not. Her last exhibition had attracted some press. The wheelchair was an irresistible visual 'point of difference'. A new tragic story about an old car crash. But the story has a happy ending. This person made it out alive. She's creating art. People are buying it. She's fine. To Lauretta's credit, the gallery promoted both Jess' previous exhibition and this one without a single wheelchair reference. But it was hard to control the story. Both official and social media had their own ideas, and her paraplegia took all of two seconds to become the headlines, taglines and first words in an article or post.

'Stop complaining, Jessica,' mother had said. 'I bet other artists are jealous of your coverage. Their personal tragedy is not that newsworthy. You can make money out of yours, lucky you.' Then she paused before adding, 'Well, *some* money.'

Kelly had said, 'The great thing is, when people see your work…I mean, really see it…they are in it. It's all about the art and them. It's no longer about you.'

'Thanks, Kel,' she smiled. 'It's what every artwork aims to do, isn't it? For the artist to become unseen.'

'Yep. Even Andy Warhol,' Kelly said, then added, 'But Frida Kahlo…'

'Don't get me started on Frida Kahlo.'

'Don't get *me* started on Frida Kahlo.'

'If only she didn't have that tram accident.'

'I know,' Kelly said. 'We'd all be feeling less pain.'

Jess stayed at the back of the room but smiled in a pained introvert-hostess way at those who looked in her direction. They smiled awkwardly back, then turned to look at the art or to continue speaking with a friend.

'They want to talk to you,' Kelly said. 'They're just worried about giving you COVID, that's all. Lauretta will start bringing them over.'

Jess had to admit, there was an increase in friendly chatter, laughter and hugging in the room. Her nervous system gave a tickle buzz when she saw those stages of people beginning to look. First: *'Photograph?'*, then closer: *'Painting?'*, then leaning in: *'WTF? Collage??'*. It was hard to see if anything was selling yet as the desk was in the middle of the gallery, surrounded by the standing masses. Just as Kelly predicted, Lauretta began appearing with an interested buyer in tow to introduce them to Jess. As usual, they wouldn't know whether to look down and yell, bend down, squat, or kneel. But Jess smiled and eased the disquiet with a 'Whatever makes you comfortable'. It's tempting to say, 'I'd rather not talk to your crotch.' Being in a place that's loud, without chairs, and you are going to talk for more than a couple of minutes, Jess figured you might as well meet at eye level by kneeling or squatting. Unless you are wearing a tight pencil skirt, like Lauretta's, who hadn't thought ahead. Some irritating access advocates on social media proclaimed that "people in wheelchairs find others squatting or kneeling patronising". This didn't help things. But Jess didn't dare wade into that snake pit with her own view. She picked her battles.

Breaking through a group of cool-looking accountants (their spectacles optometry prêt-à-porter) was a man who looked more comfortable than anyone else there. Which was an achievement, as he was alone. Or seemed to be. Jess observed the scene. She noticed the man's elegant dusting of grey in his short brown hair, trimmed grey stubble and toned biceps through his red t-shirt. His tanned skin, rolled-out-of-bed hair and easy poise made him look like an off-duty surf lifesaver. Jess sniffed in high alert when he stopped to look at her personal favourite, the *TV* artwork, just near where Kelly and Jess had positioned themselves. One thing about him was hard to miss. He was in an electric wheelchair, but not just any electric wheelchair.

'Pride Jazzy Air 2.0,' Jess murmured.

'That's one way to describe him,' Kelly replied. They both watched, mesmerised, as his chair slowly rose to greet the artwork at 'head height', inspecting the prison warden looking at the prisoner looking at the television.

'One touch air elevation,' Jess whispered. 'Adjustable suspension.'

'You have to get one of those. The wheelchair or the guy. Doesn't matter.'

'I think they come as a package,' she replied. He was so close. Paying such deep attention to the detail, he was practically fogging up the Perspex sheet protecting the artwork. Like mixing red paint in water, a fast-spreading blush took over Jess' pale face.

'Shit,' said Kelly.

'What?'

'He's drinking orange juice. Where the hell did he get that?' Kelly stormed off to catering for answers.

Minutes passed before he drew back from his absorbed state and turned to look at Jess, to whom he gave a gentle smile and a nod. It was like that between people in wheelchairs. Jess reminded herself. Like how bus drivers wave to each other while passing en route. Jess nodded back. He lowered himself back to seat height and made his way towards her. Jess knew that the Pride Jazzy allowed him to make his way to her at full height, but he had lowered himself to her level out of politeness. Or it was for fear of being knocked over by the large, gesticulating woman nearby whose sparkling wine had been topped up one too many times. Jess couldn't be sure.

'Biscuit Chickens,' Jess said when he sat before her. She was reading the words on the man's t-shirt. 'What does that mean?'

'Absolutely nothing,' he replied with a grin.

'Maybe it means something to the Asian company that manufactured it,' she laughed. 'A culture gap?'

'No, I made it,' he said. 'Well, I typed the words on this t-shirt design platform, and someone else made it and posted it to me. Probably from China.'

Then Jess saw it. The t-shirt was the perfect icebreaker. Shifting the attention away from the wheelchair, it started a conversation on something stupid and funny. 'I want one,' she said.

'I'm afraid not. This is a unique, a one-off. You need to think of your own words. I'd be happy to organise it for you, though.'

'Oh no, I'm not good with words.'

'Give it a go. Just off the top of your head.' Her brain went into meltdown while scrolling through words. *Biscuit chicken… cake…something…lizard…bloody speed poetry.* 'Muffin… ducks?'

'Muffin ducks is perfect,' he said. Jess noticed his slightly crooked teeth and smiled. Nature had saved the man from being too good-looking. A wabi-sabi of the face. 'Not a great deal of effort involved, as opposed to this,' he gestured towards *TV*. Mim, the gallery assistant, appeared to put a round black sticker on the artwork's label. With shaved head and nose piercings, Mim still somehow managed to look like the love child of a surf champion and a Disney princess. She smiled across at him with perfect teeth before diving back into the ocean of bodies.

'Did you just buy that?' Kelly reappeared, kitchen now fully in line with protocol.

'Me?' he asked, startled. 'No, I wouldn't…'

'Why? You don't like it?' Kelly frowned defensively, as if it were her own work. Before, Jess wanted to blend into the wall. Now she wanted to sink through the concrete flooring until she hit Earth's core.

'It's brilliant,' he replied. 'But it's so sad. So lonely. I couldn't live with it. It belongs in an art museum. What's the one here?'

'NGV,' Jess and Kelly said in unison.

'See, what do I know? I live here, I grew up here and don't even know the name of the main art gallery. I'm going to shut up now.'

'Not so fast,' Kelly said, raising her finger. 'Of all the work in the exhibition, which one would you be happiest to live with?'

'You don't have to answer that,' Jess interjected.

'No, it's a good question. Gee, I don't know. Maybe the one of you with the camera,' he said, nodding to Kelly. 'That's a keeper.' She responded with a proud smile, as if it were her own work. Jess cleared her throat for attention. Then she wished she hadn't, sore throats and coughing being COVID symptoms.

'This is the artist, Jessica Adams.'

'Really? I thought it was this one,' he said, giving a side look to Kelly. 'Well, congratulations, Jessica. I hope my comments didn't offend. I–'

'Not at all.' Jess almost touched his arm to reassure, then retreated.

'It's an extraordinary exhibition. And something that's obviously made with hands, not on a screen. We're all so sick of screens.'

Both paper-based artists beamed at him in gratitude, but then Kelly groaned. Jess' mother had arrived.

Curly red hair, orange frangipani print muumuu and a plethora of wooden beads all fought with each other as she beelined towards them. 'Darling, how wonderful to see this turnout. That said, no one seems to care about their health anymore. Or yours,' she delivered with a sage nod. 'Too many people can be a problem. Not just COVID. You can't see the work. Any hint of sales, no?'

'Yes, actually–' Jess started, pointing across to *TV*.

Imogen stared at Jess' empty wine glass. 'Should you be drinking, darling? It's important to keep tidy tonight.' She swiftly lifted Jess' glass out of her hand and placed it on a passing tray.

Kelly interjected. 'Aren't you supposed to be home, Imogen? COVID symptoms?'

'Thank you for your concern, Kelly, but my symptoms have vanished completely. Mild to begin with. I was being overly cautious. Feeling one hundred percent now. And so, naturally, as my daughter needs my support, I thought I'd better hotfoot it down here. And…who…might…this…be?' Imogen spoke slowly to the man, bending over to face him, as if staring at an insect on a flower. Jess began to carry out introductions, then realised she didn't know Biscuit Chickens' true identity.

Unperturbed by the peering woman, the man smiled. 'I'm Scott. Lovely to meet the mother of this amazing artist. You must be very proud.'

Imogen straightened up, almost offended that the man spoke articulately. 'With all the time Jessica spends on each work,' she waved with abandon, 'you would hope some good came out of it.'

Kelly saw her friend's chest deflate. 'Jess needs to talk to some buyers, Imogen. Let me give you the tour.'

'We mustn't impede a sale. Even if all it does is cover the outrageous framing costs.' She then did a double-take. 'Biscuit Chickens?' But Kelly was already leading Imogen towards the vicinity of the cool accountants. 'Kelly, will you make sure everyone's social distancing, please?' Kelly looked back towards Jess and Scott and made a strangulation gesture around her own neck before continuing.

Scott laughed, 'Our mothers could go head-to-head.'

'Really? You have one of these, too?'

'Mothers can be overly protective as a rule, right? If you are in a wheelchair, they get crazy-protective, even when you're a fully-fledged adult,' he said. 'Particularly if it happened young. I was fourteen years old, playing an under-15's football game.'

She didn't say 'I'm sorry.' That's what other people said, the standing. Instead, she offered, 'Six years old, freak car accident.' It was not a competition of who was worse off. It was fast tracking comradery through sharing war stories.

He nodded, then said, 'I'm T9 complete.'

'Me too!' she smiled, as if they had been to the same concert or had the same favourite food. They had the same area of spinal cord damage. Paralysis below the waist. 'Must say, I'm a bit envious of your Pride Jazzy Air.'

'I'm usually in a manual, better for bumpy terrain.' He paused, looking slightly flustered. 'But you already know about the benefits of manuals, sorry. The Jazz is a bit of a princess. Likes the smooth, flat surfaces. That said, it can be easier for meeting standing strangers.'

'That ol' chestnut,' she said. 'And it's great for looking at hanging art.'

'As it turns out, yes.'

'Your shoulders suggest manual,' she said. It was a fact, unintended to be flirty. Then she realised it was.

A subtle shift in his body language betrayed a small pleasure from the comment. 'I play some basketball,' he shrugged. 'Do you play sport?'

Jess sensed this was more his comfort zone, not art. 'I'm not really competitive.' She almost apologised but stopped short.

Kelly had been policing her apologies as part of her assertiveness program. 'I've been getting into yoga lately. It's been good for my state of mind around the exhibition.' She laughed, then realised she probably sounded mentally unstable. A second realisation dawned. He probably has a girlfriend. Maybe a wife. Children. Jesus. Looking over his shoulder, she asked, 'Come with anyone, friends?'

'I was supposed to. This guy from my team was going to come. He was the one who knew about tonight and invited me along. Loves your work but bailed at the last minute. He wanted to stay home, even after all those lockdowns. I guess some need to ease their way back out.' Scott's expression turned earnest. 'I'd better leave you to it. Your friend said you need to talk with buyers? I wish I could afford one of your works, but...'

'Please, no. That's not -,' Jess flustered. 'It's just so great talking...'

The gallery director tottered her way towards them, dragging a woman behind her dressed in what appeared to be a fashionable pink garbage bag. A man dressed in black was following them, carrying a camera Kelly would envy. Serious media. Scott pulled away. 'You are in demand, unsurprisingly. Really great to meet you, Jessica.' She wanted to ask for his number, but the confidence just wouldn't come. Instead, like a lump, she watched him expertly negotiate moving obstacles, weaving through inebriated art lovers as he headed towards the door. Damn that fine-tuned VR2 joystick controller.

She turned to see the plastic bag woman's face in front of hers, body all bent and contorted, poised to ask her first question. Jessica got in first. 'Muffin ducks,' she said.

'*Upcycle Artist on Wheels Ramps up Art Scene*', Kelly read out from *The Age* newspaper the weekend after the exhibition. Plastic garbage bag woman decided environmental sustainability was the angle for the exhibition, besides the paraplegia. 'Was she drunk when she wrote this?'

'If she wrote it at the exhibition, probably. Everyone was so hammered it's a miracle the art wasn't knocked off the walls.'

'It was no miracle that you have already sold over half the exhibition,' Kelly said. 'And that the NGV bought *TV*. That's sheer talent, my friend.'

'Selling to the NGV was something, wasn't it?' Jess grinned. 'Thank you,' she said as a waiter plonked a long black down in front of her. A tiger tattoo covered his arm, its ample bottom featuring just below the shirt sleeve.

It was Saturday. Kelly had declared a celebratory brunch. Jess suggested a café around the corner from the gallery, as she planned to drop in to see Lauretta afterwards.

'You're not going to the gallery after this,' Kelly said.

'I just wanted to pop in…'

'No, Lauretta told you she will be in touch when there is something to say. Leave her alone to do her job. Now, let's eat,' she said. 'Shame about the smell in here.'

Jess looked up and sniffed, 'What smell?'

'The smell of cool urban café desperation. Aren't you tired of the design formula?' Kelly waved her hand towards the white subway tiles, well-marked blackboards and recycled timber shelves stocked with absurdly priced preserves. Staff chicaned around tables wearing immaculate navy linen aprons with dark leather strapping.

Male staff wore full beards behind their navy linen masks. Regardless of gender, a cacophony of tattoos was on every staff member's person.

'We've all just come out of lockdown, Kel. Be grateful.'

They did their best to converse over the crunching, grinding, banging and hissing of the coffee machine. The summer heat was closing in, but a slight breeze drifted through like a languid socialite. Comforting aromas of artisan sourdough toast and free trade coffee made the battle for a wheelchair accessible table, or any table, worthwhile. But Kelly noticed her friend wasn't as perky as expected.

'I know,' she said, reaching out to touch Jess' hand. 'Just because they say, "organic free range," doesn't mean the chicken is happy about the situation.'

Jess cracked a smile. 'Sorry. It's just…there's a guy going to town on me on Instagram because of the sustainability claims of that article. The very thing I was afraid of.'

'You have a troll?' Kelly asked, her body already steeling itself to launch into combat. 'Who is this bastard?'

'squintman20.' Jess scrolled her phone. 'Here it is. He says as a comment to the article, "*Sustainable, my arse. Jessica Adams' framing is plantation timber mould, painted with white acrylic. That's plastic, people. Non-reflective acrylic sheeting, which–I'd put money on–isn't recycled. Plastic, plastic, plastic.*" I never called myself a sustainability artist. Or an upcycle artist or an eco-artist.'

'So the genius knows his framing materials. And it's bloody expensive plastic, so the works last. It is also true you make your collages of…' Kelly turned back to the newspaper article, "…*fragmented upcycled paper.*"'

'Otherwise known as cut or ripped bits of old magazine,' Jess said. She had a trusted contact at a Lifeline charity shop who sourced old magazines for her.

Kelly continued to read the article. '"*The paper elements…*" Wow, that's even wankier than paper fragments, "*…were adhered using environmentally friendly, vegan glue on one hundred percent recycled, unbleached, acid-free Forest Stewardship Council-certified board while achieving optimum quality control for artwork longevity.*" All of which we know to be true.'

Over the years, Jess had worked out that these materials would reliably hold together, even in direct sunlight, for the best part of the day. The non-reflective acrylic sheeting had UV protection. It was all tried and tested. The work had to be of museum standard. An artwork that falls apart after a couple of years is a career death kiss.

'As we had discussed many times, an unpainted recycled timber frame would be Sunday market poxy,' Kelly said. 'And glass instead of Perspex is pointless. You can't see the work at all.' She took a sip of her latte. 'Clearly, squintman20 lacks 20-20 vision on the matter.'

Jess appreciated Kelly's understanding about the framing, given her passion for environmental conservation. But Kelly had a similar challenge. Photography processing usually meant chemicals. Lots of chemicals. Googling together, they found a fine art print lab that used paper made out of the pure recycled cotton remnants from cottonseed oil manufacturers. The inks were water-based, lightfast pigments. Their studio was carbon neutral.

'Pretty pricey though,' Kelly said.

'You can bypass the cost of framing by hanging your sheets using those small wall magnets.'

'Which looks art-cool, right?' Kelly smiled as she swivelled in her chair. Then her smile dropped, and the swivelling stopped. 'Are magnets environmentally friendly?'

'Absolutely,' Jess said. 'Except what they are made of. And how they are made. And if you don't throw them out.'

'No problem then,' Kelly reclined back in her chair, frowning as she stared out the window at a sky patched up with clouds.

'Oh, my god. He was there,' Jess said. Kelly put down *The Age* and slid her chair towards Jess' to look at her phone. 'That's us at the opening.'

'Nothing is sacred when you are an art star.'

'I look worried,' Jess said.

'You were worried,' Kelly replied. 'It was early. No one was drunk yet.'

'True. You look happy though.'

'I was happy.'

'I'd just told you mum wasn't coming to the opening.'

'Funny how the mood flipped for both of us during the evening,' Kelly said. 'Anyhoo, what does squint-n-squirt say about us?'

'Fake sustainability artist, Jessica Adams.'

'Really? Both of us are Jessica Adams?' she gasped. 'Interesting how the photo doesn't show you are in a wheelchair.'

'I just look short.'

'Or I look tall.' Kelly said, taking the phone. 'Despite the crap composition, it's a decent photo. Not a phone shot. Weird.' Kelly shook her head, then scrolled. 'No photos of him on his own account, did you notice?'

'Look at his profile image. That's him, right? He looks like Van Gogh but in better days,' she said, 'wearing a jaunty hat.'

'That jaunty hat belongs to Ansel Adams, the face too. Squintman's in hiding. What a gutless wonder.' Then Kelly's eyes widened as she looked up at Jess. 'Are you related to Ansel Adams? Is that why he's stalking you? You would have told me you're related to Ansel Adams, right? Squintman's clearly jealous. As am I. Man, what a genius photographer. Oh my God, Jess. Why didn't you tell me?'

'Calm down, Kel. I'm not related to Ansel Adams. Or Bryan, Amy, or Douglas Adams or the Addams Family.'

Kelly took a breath as Jess handed her a glass of water. Kelly drained the glass and then sighed, staring out over the brunchers. 'Okay, so what are we going to say in response to Squatman?'

'WE are not saying anything.' Jess took the phone back. 'Let's not start art wars.'

'This guy's taking shots at you… and of you. Sis, we've got to take him down.'

Jess rubbed at her forehead. 'I think we should sit on it. He'll probably get bored, move onto someone else.'

'I could go after him as me,' Kelly said, taking out her phone. 'You don't have to be involved.'

'But I am involved,' she said. 'I appreciate it, Kel. But please just leave it for now.'

'Okay, it's your call,' she said. 'But if he keeps going, we're doing something.'

'Okay.'

'Speaking of distracting men, any word from Mr Jazz?'

'Mr Jazz?' Jess furrowed her brow. 'Oh, you mean Scott of the Pride Jazzy Air 2.0. No, garbage bag woman ambushed us. He slipped away before I could suggest catching up again.'

'Because you were going to do that. You are that smooth.'

'Shut up and eat your eggs benny.'

Jess dropped into the gallery a few days later, upon invitation. Lauretta had said there's a package to collect, and that she had some good news.

Today, the gallery director was wearing black pants with a floral silk shirt. She was crouch-ready, but there was no need. They were both sitting comfortably in her office while Mim attended the gallery desk. The office was almost as minimalist as the gallery. White desk, Mac computer, chrome desk lamp. One small wall was lined with a chest-height white cube bookshelf jammed with art books. Standard chest height, not Jess chest height. Above the shelves hung a work by Jess from her previous exhibition. In fact, it was three small works hung together as a story about a girl going outside. The first was inside with a small, warm lamp light. The second was of the girl at a doorway looking out. Then the third in a lush garden and sunshine. Lauretta bought them before anyone else could. This was a significant compliment, as she rarely bought artworks herself. 'I spend all day with art,' she explained once with a flap of her hand. The three collages were symbolic of the exhibition itself. Jess, who had been alone in her creativity bubble, was now outside. She was seen and appreciated, not just by the buyers, but by many walks of life.

'I really need to take that triptych home.' Lauretta said. 'People keep wanting it for themselves.'

'It's nice to see it again,' Jess said. 'Interesting how the past makes you think about the future. I'm not sure what I'm going to work on next.'

'It'll come. You earned a break,' she said. 'The good news is you have another sell-out show. Well done.' Lauretta was beaming. 'Look out for more money in your bank account by tomorrow. I've emailed you the breakdown of amounts against which works.'

'Really? Those last ones sold?' The news floored Jess. The incessant worry of moving back in with her mother immediately lifted. She would've dropped to the floor and kissed the polished concrete if it wasn't such a bother getting back up again.

'Mim's putting up the last of the black dots now. We held back until you arrived.' Lauretta looked at Jess sideways. 'You seem shocked.'

'Well, I wondered whether that Squintman guy online would be successful in his systematic attack on my credibility. It's been going for days, and people are buying into it. You can tell by their comments. It's bizarre. I keep telling Kelly it's fine, but is it?'

'Yes, and as I told you a couple of days ago, trolls are wherever successful people are. It's a kind of weird compliment. Pulling pigtails. People like that will say anything to get a response. But engaging with him will just exacerbate the behaviour. You can see the man is deranged. That's why we haven't replied to the claims. I have taken screenshots, just in case. But it's not worth reporting at this stage. I wouldn't worry about it.'

But Jess was worried. That morning, he messaged directly a photo of her and Kelly sitting at breakfast that last Saturday. The troll had become a stalker. She chose not to show Kelly, as it would trigger social media fireworks. But she showed Lauretta.

'Creepy,' Lauretta admitted. 'But it's not illegal to take a photo of someone in public. He is still within his rights.' She looked harder at the photo. 'It's quite a good quality image. He could publish this,' she said. 'Okay, send me the photo, when he took it and when he sent it. I'll let the local police know as a heads-up, but they won't be able to do anything. In the meantime, block him across Facebook, Messenger and Instagram and leave it at that. The key to surviving stuff like this is to ignore it.'

Jess pulled out her phone and texted Lauretta the image and date details. 'I'm so happy the whole exhibition has sold, but this guy...' she said as she blocked Squintman across all platforms. 'Okay, that's all done. Thanks, Lauretta.'

'Get your mind off it. Open your package,' she said, passing over the small, flimsy plastic package addressed to Jess, along with some scissors. Jess looked at the sender's address. It was a Melbourne PO Box she didn't recognise. There was also a cool-looking logo touting the mystery acronym 'SM'.

'Squintman has branding?'

Lauretta laughed, then frowned. 'Surely not. Do you want me to open it?'

'No, it's okay,' she replied. 'Let's just hope it's not a bomb or anthrax.' Pulling out some taupe-green fabric, she laughed when she saw what it was. A t-shirt with the white words 'Muffin Duck' printed in a classic font best suited to boutique investment banks. 'What a lovely colour.' Holding it up to her body, she said, 'I think he got my size right.'

'Muffin Duck?' Lauretta asked.

'It's from Scott. The guy at the opening wearing the red t-shirt saying Biscuit Chickens? Remember him, in the wheelchair?'

Lauretta nodded, 'Vaguely.'

'I asked him what Biscuit Chickens meant. And he said that it didn't mean anything. Then I said...'

'I get it,' Lauretta replied, holding up her hand. Her phone was ringing. 'Sorry, gotta take this.'

When Jess rolled the t-shirt so it could fit in her handbag, she noticed a card with a SmartMerchie logo, which explained the 'SM' logo. It was the manufacturer's brand. The card had a typed message on it. *'Your unique t-shirt, another original by Jessica Adams. Hope it starts some great conversations, Scott Wicks.'* Following Scott's name was his phone number. Jess grinned and blushed and snorted all at the same time. Lauretta was still deep in conservation of one-syllable words. 'Yes… no. Fine… well… I… yes… I can…' Jess caught Lauretta's eye with a wave and gestured she was leaving. Lauretta gave a thumbs up, then blew her a kiss. Wheeling through the gallery, she thanked Mim, who returned with a broad smile and two thumbs up (black nail polish, perfectly manicured), then headed for the street. Feeling the warmth of the dappled sunshine playing amongst the London plane tree leaves, Jess made her way towards the beach for one more look before heading home to stalk Scott on social media.

He had a Facebook profile, but there wasn't much to see. Scott with his basketball team after they won a game; Scott in a restaurant celebrating someone's birthday with a group of smiling faces above a dangerous array of cocktails; Scott at a football match holding a beer, looking concerned for his team. She stopped scrolling when she spotted Scott with a woman sitting at a picnic table from about six months ago. The woman was not in a wheelchair. She was very attractive. Naturally attractive, not Botox-and-fake-eyelashes attractive. Jess felt a surge of jealousy, which was ridiculous. 'I barely know the guy,' she told herself, shaking her head. She kept scrolling. Other than those personal photos, his posts were mostly of animals doing stupid things. Jess couldn't help but get sucked into those and almost cried while watching the casually sauntering lion accidentally falling into a lake. One post was putting the word out to help a friend find Doug, their missing dog. Doug was found. "Call off the dogs!" Scott said. He had also shared a post from Beyond Blue for those suffering from depression or anxiety during COVID. 'What a guy,' she murmured to herself. Jess was also impressed by the video of a dinosaur at the UN giving a speech against extinction. But that was it. It seemed Scott had no Instagram, LinkedIn or Twitter profile. And not a Biscuit Chicken in sight.

They met for a drink at a bar with an outdoor area, just to be COVID-safe-ish. Both agreed to wear their t-shirts. Jess' fitted perfectly, which was remarkable given her extensive experience with online shopping. When you are in a wheelchair, shopping for clothes is a pain. The stairs and escalators are one thing. Fitting into changing rooms was a whole other ballgame. Then it's the actual trying on of clothes, which can take forever. Online shopping is the answer, and Jess became a gold standard expert in sizing, as well as in button and zipper placement.

'Thanks again for Muffin Duck. I love it.' She raised her glass of Pino Gris. Scott met hers with his can of Moon Dog IPA. He was in his manual chair this time. Simple, light and foldable.

'The t-shirt looks great on you,' he grinned. 'Hope it makes people laugh.'

'Me too. People need a laugh. COVID has been...' Jess didn't need to finish the sentence. Discussing COVID first up had become a kind of necessary ritual for everyone in the community. It had to be brought up so you could move on from it.

'I know,' Scott said. 'Unable to dance. Having to sit while drinking or eating...'

'Working from home...' Jess said. 'Wait, that's what I do every day.'

'We're so stoic.' Scott chuckled. Jess enjoyed looking at Scott's face. Noticing the pieces of it, as if he were a collage. The distinct tones in his grey stubble beard, in his skin, his blue eyes with flecks of light brown. 'Yeah, working from home was fine for me,' he continued. 'I'm at the uni, RMIT, in admin. It's easy to do anywhere as long as you can log in. Not as exciting as your job.'

'My job ripping up bits of paper, then sticking them together for hours on end?'

'It's more than that, I can tell. There's this whole creative process happening.'

'Sometimes it can be boring once I've worked out what I'm doing. Thank god for podcasts.'

'What are you listening to?'

'Lately, just a lot of art podcasts. It's amazing how good they are, given how many artists are introverts. We communicate through our work, not through microphones. I hate being interviewed.'

'I have to admit, I googled you. Saw some great articles about your work.'

'Thanks,' she said. 'You didn't look on social media, by any chance?'

'No, I'm pretty crap at that. My friends laugh at me about my old man ways. But I should get back on Facebook and support you. Like and share and stuff.'

'No, please don't do that on my behalf. Save yourself!' Jess laughed. 'It's just that there's this guy who's been trolling me. Saying that I've been promoting myself falsely as an environmental artist. But that wasn't me. It was a journalist who called me environmental. He was at the opening but didn't introduce himself.

Instead, he posted a photo of Kelly and me hanging out at the back of the gallery. Then he direct messaged a photo of Kelly and me having breakfast a few days later.'

'Jesus,' he said. 'This guy isn't just a troll, he's a stalker.' Scott's expression matched the one he had at the football on Facebook. Grave concern with beer can suspended. There was no doubt it was genuine.

'Stalker-lite,' Jess said, feeling slightly guilty about going through Scott's socials like someone in forensics.

'What's his name? I can track him down...' he said, then stopped. 'What is it? You look-'

'It's...well...,' Jess faltered, processing her feelings. 'I guess I'm not used to male protectiveness. Just Kelly. And, I guess, mum and Lauretta at the gallery.'

'Your dad?' Scott asked.

'Died in the car accident, along with my little brother.'

'I am so sorry. God, that's awful.'

'It happened a long time ago. A freak accident. No one's fault.'

'Perhaps it goes some way to explaining your mum trying extra-hard to keep you under her wing.'

'It's hard when you're in your thirties.' Jess almost said 'late thirties' but saved herself just in time.

'Tell me about it. Wait until you meet mine,' Scott laughed, then looked horrified. 'Sorry, I meant that as a turn of phrase.' Jess was delighted to meet someone as awkward as her, but as attractive as him. 'No, it's fine. I'd love to see our mothers together. Maybe they will become obsessed with each other and leave us alone.'

'Or they will combine to become a mother superpower. Then we'll never escape.'

'We'd better play it safe,' she said.

'Talking of playing it safe, who is this stalker?'

'We don't know his real name. Squintman20 is his handle,' she said. 'He has no photos of himself.'

'Coward.'

'Trolls and stalkers usually are, right?' she said. Scott shrugged in agreement. 'Lauretta understands the legals better than I do. She's notified the police, but they can't do anything. Apparently, the best tactic is to block and ignore. So that's what I'm doing. The exhibition has sold well, which apparently entitles me to a break now.'

'You're on holidays?' Scott took a sip of his beer and settled back in his chair. 'That's great.'

'For as long as an artist can be. The works take so long to make, I should get back into it as soon as possible,' she said. 'I did have a job working as an assembler at a curtain rod factory. And I was pretty good at it too, I might add.'

'I have no doubt,' Scott replied.

'But I really wanted to make it as an artist. Just before COVID, I took the leap.'

'So to speak.'

'So to speak,' she tilted her glass towards him. 'Living off art sales and a small pension.'

'Sounds like it's paying off.'

'We sold out the exhibition,' she said with a sudden shyness.

'Sold out completely?' he asked, almost yelling. 'Jess, I should be buying you champagne!'

'That's very sweet of you, but I like my Pino Gris.'

'Dinner then?'

'Oh, okay,' she said, surprised. 'Sounds great. When?'

'Tomorrow night?'

'Tomorrow night?' Jess didn't expect such a quick turnaround.

'You're right,' he said. 'It might not be enough time to organise my evening shirt with Macaroon Gecko on it.'

'Tomorrow night it is,' she smiled. 'Without conversation starters.'

When Jess went home that evening, something was amiss. She had let herself into her ground-floor, one-bedroom unit, feeling upbeat about the sales and dinner with Scott. On the way home, a sense of possibility began trickling into her consciousness. She dared herself to imagine having a second bedroom to use as a studio, rather than the dining room table. Or even rent proper studio space in an artist collective. But the thought of loud music and chatter made her backtrack on that idea. 'Home studio,' she said to herself, 'with proper shelving and a bigger table. And maybe a Pride Jazzy Air 2.0.'

Coming through the front door, she turned on the lights. The entry was straight into the lounge-dining area, looking into the open kitchen of white, chrome and a feature splashback in apple green. Small timber side tables flanked the grey-blue couch with red and orange cushions. A central coffee table would get in the way. Jess had arranged the furniture with enough space to move around in her chair. One of Kelly's photographic images hung above the couch in a box timber frame. It was a close-up of a drooping she-oak branch coming into view from the left. The grey-blue ocean was on the right in the background.

'It's a female she-oak,' Kelly explained later. 'You can see the small red flowers hanging down to catch the male pollen from the nearby male she-oak.'

'Really?' Jess was a little shocked at how often she had looked at an image she knew so little about. 'Maybe I should've hung it in the bedroom.'

Then she saw it. Something small and torn on her white-washed timber dining table. A photo? She didn't remember leaving anything there. In fact, she'd made a point of clearing all remnants of the exhibition so she could enjoy the dining table as a dining table for the first time in over a year. She was planning to have Kelly over, treat her to a home-cooked meal to thank her for being such a first-class friend through the whole exhibition palaver.

Jess moved closer to the table and saw it was a photo, ripped into pieces and scattered. There was no need to jigsaw it. She already knew it was the family photo, the last one taken before the accident. They were on her uncle's boat with lifejackets on. Jess recalled her brother being a whining pain in the arse that day and her father promising ice-cream later as appeasement. This was the photo she kept in a frame by her bed. Seeing it scattered across the table, a black heaviness came over her and sank into her organs. The urge to both cry and vomit became almost overwhelming. It felt like her skin had been torn off her body, her nerve endings bare. But there was another strange feeling. A truth. Her mind also recognised what was before her as art. Torn to bits, it said everything about the true condition of her family since that time.

'The word "sustainability" is a weird word, isn't it? When nothing stays the same,' a male voice said behind her.

Turning around as fast as her chair would allow, she saw a stranger. In a daze, she took in what she could: a man in his thirties, maybe. Sandy hair, jeans, black t-shirt. But the wild look in his eye, framed by thick, black-rimmed glasses, was an unmistakable message. Jess pulled back a half-wheel.

Seeing a burglar in your home is a shock. But a burglar in a wheelchair was confounding. The chair was a sports manual, designed for basketball, with the wheels tilted inwards. For these chairs, you need quick hands and strength to stop and change direction. He looked like he probably had that covered. The chair was also fine for moving fast within the confines of Jess' unit.

'Squintman?' she asked, though it was more of a whisper.

'That's Squintman20 to you,' he laughed as he affected a squint. The gesture was moronic, which made him seem more unhinged and threatening.

'What do you want?' she asked, almost yelling now. 'What have I done to you?'

'You think you're so smart?' he spat. 'So successful. And that being in a chair means nothing.'

'Not really…' she replied, perplexed. Then it became clear. This guy didn't need a reason. He was angry, and he had chosen her as the target. An easy target.

'You and your Muffin Duck and Scott with bloody Biscuit Chickens. All very nice and cosy,' he said with a sneer.

'You know Scott? You're the basketball friend?' Jess said this as she tried to roll backwards into the kitchen. The space was smaller, less accessible. A place with weapons.

'You would never have met him if it wasn't for me,' he yelled as he lunged towards her. Before she knew it, he was grabbing her by her t-shirt and pulling her down with him as he fell to the floor. Wheelchairs crashed around them. She could hear the Muffin Duck fabric rip in his grip, which converted her fear into fury. Jess had training in some simple self-defence moves for paraplegics when she was a teen. Her teacher thought it could help with building confidence. It didn't really work. Jess' self-doubt seemed impregnable. But the repetitious exercises had somehow stuck in her psyche. In seconds, she was deftly pulling Squintman's index and middle fingers apart and bending the wrist backwards. He was strong and had his other hand at her throat. While she still had air, she punched his throat as hard as she could. The back of his head smacked on the corner of a protruding wall, dividing the kitchen from the hallway. He groaned and released his grip for a moment, then got it back. She pulled off his glasses and tried to stab him in the eye with them, but he got her wrist fixed in his grip. Punching him in the armpit surprised him enough for her to roll her body away, but he dragged up behind her and grabbed her around the waist. She used her elbow to strike him in the gut, then at his temple. He was flat on his back, dazed, so she punched him in the throat again. Hard. Twice. He was breathing, but unmoved. Dragging herself into the kitchen, she found packing tape in the lowest drawer and dragged herself back to bind his hands. Legs weren't necessary. Mouth was not a priority. After crawling away from him, she noticed her hands were trembling. He moaned and half-rolled while Jess found her phone in her bag and called 000 for an emergency response. After giving a shaken debrief, she stayed on the line until the police and ambulance arrived.

'Trevor Miles,' Scott said. 'I would never have picked it. I'm so sorry, Jess. He seemed so nice. A demon on the court, but we all are. Or at least try to be.' Jess had phoned Scott the next day to cancel dinner. She was no longer in a celebratory mood. Scott then groaned. 'He showed me his photography. People in crowds. The photos looked great... Jesus.'

'The weird thing is, he is an excellent photographer. Kelly says he needs to learn how to use a camera for good and not evil.'

'Sure does,' he said. 'Even though Trevor's confessed, I'll call the police to give a statement. If you want, I can get a re-print of Muffin Duck?'

Jess paused. The police had taken the ripped t-shirt as evidence, with Jess' blessing. That was before the paramedic had checked her over and took early photos of bruising. 'I think I need new words,' she said.

'Fair enough. No hurry.'

'He was right about one thing,' she said. 'We wouldn't have met if it weren't for him.'

'I'm grateful for that,' he said. 'I just wish I had been there last night. Did someone stay with you after the police left?'

'Yes, Kelly was with me. She's amazing, as always. Squint... Trevor broke in from around the back,' she said. 'The lock on that door's been tricky lately. The locksmith came around last night to sort it so I could sleep.'

'Did you sleep?'

'Not really. I might take a nap soon,' she said, watching Kelly washing up the breakfast dishes.

Today, Kelly was still on guard for Jess. Not against Squintman, as he was in custody. But from Imogen, who was determined Jess was moving back in with her.

'I'm fine, Mum,' Jess had said. 'Stronger than ever.' Which was true in one way. She felt exhausted, bruised, and still a little shaky. But Jess also recognised that she was tougher than she knew. That she was no sitting duck.

Kelly was leaving soon, at Jess' request, but was coming back for dinner. 'How about I bring around some takeaway for the three of us after work?' Scott suggested.

'That sounds great,' she said, and it did. Then she had it. 'Gingernut Dragon,' she said. 'On hot pink, same font. Would that be doable?'

'Of course,' Scott laughed. 'Anything else?'

'When you come over tonight, can you bring a packet of Twisties?'

'Given how I eat those things once I start,' he said, 'I'm going to have to bring a family pack.' Jess laughed while feeling the pain from her bruising. The good and the bad together. Humour and aching. Attempted murder and accidental matchmaking. Being kick-ass and vulnerable. Having the whole and the torn.

CALL WAITING

[Organic Oatmeal Cookie]

Fleur smacked her ear. Then she slapped her palm hard on the laminated café table. Her latté glass jumped. People turned to look at her, but all Fleur's attention was on the mosquito. She could either hear the mosquito or see the mosquito, but never simultaneously. When going for the kill, the insect disappeared completely. Eventually, it would reappear somewhere else. This was nature's magic trick. Much of her life had become elusive since moving to the country. She had found herself both homeless and unemployed, and discovered that the two work naturally together.

Like many urban dwellers, Fleur wasn't sure about nature. But two months before, while swivelling behind the desk of a contemporary art gallery, the idea of it had been appealing.

'Girl, you need a solid game plan,' said Meera. Meera was a brilliant mid-career artist who had earned her stripes. Her paintings, depicting Australian natives in a traditional Indian flat-pattern style, graced the walls of many stylish Sydney homes. But she worked as a mental health art therapist at the hospital to supplement her income. Meera had the pragmatism of a siege strategist. 'You can't just go up there without a job and digs lined up. Regional Australia is not always as pretty as it looks.'

'Don't worry,' Fleur replied. 'I've already nabbed a mid-level administrative job at the local university. Plus, a cute rental studio nestled in a leafy two-acre property, newly renovated. Contracts for both are awaiting my signature upon my arrival. All sorted,' she smiled. 'Maybe I'll even go back to printmaking. The university has a studio there, do a bit of self-therapy.'

'Maybe,' Meera said, looking at Fleur sideways. She then shrugged. 'Maybe.'

Upon arrival, both the job and the studio had disappeared under a hum of excuses and apologies. There had been unforeseen changes that no one was in control of. *Apart from the gods*, Fleur thought, as she saw the black speck hovering about her knee. She swatted and missed.

Fleur had hated selling art for years. Even though she was excellent at it and was finally earning a decent living, it was like her soul had wandered off in search of better company. In downtime, the Sydney clubs, cafés, and restaurants Fleur could rely on to bring the yin-yang of connection and adrenaline were no longer delivering the chi needed. Even art was losing its lustre. Most of her friends were telling the same stories, treacled in the same versions of gossip, all too familiar from the day she first met them. Adam and Pete were exceptions to the rule. Which was why, when Fleur announced she was moving seven hours north, she listened patiently through their uproar.

'You're a sophisticated citified woman,' Adam had said, accompanied by a clink from his gin and tonic.

'He's right,' Pete, Adam's boyfriend, replied. 'They have insects the size of Bloomingdale's up there.'

'Pete wants us to move to New York,' Adam explained. 'It's his new thing.'

Pete turned to Fleur. 'Come with us. The place is lined with art. You'll love it.'

'I need to move to the country,' Fleur said. 'I need space.'

'Space?' Pete asked. 'You've been working in an enormous

white art gallery.' Pete threw his arm wide, the one that was holding the beer bottle. Adam yelled, 'Hey,' wiping Pete's Wild Yak froth off his face. But Pete continued, 'You've been in more space than the rest of our workplaces put together.'

'Which says a lot,' Adam intercepted, looking at Pete sideways, 'coming from a man who works in a cubicle.'

'I need *natural* space,' she clarified.

Pete paused. 'You're in your mid-thirties, sister. That's way too young to retire to some backwater. You don't even have children.'

'I don't even have a husband, so I'm free to do whatever I want,' she replied.

'I'm too old to move to a new country, dear one,' Adam mumbled to Pete, 'except maybe Tahiti.'

'Adam, you are fifty-four. That's not too old.' Pete turned to Fleur and whispered loudly, 'Someday I'm going to make it in New York.'

'Make what?' Adam asked.

'Make New Yorkers happy as a creative, expressive human being.'

'Because they just don't have enough of those already, do they?'

'They don't have me,' Pete took a sip of his Yak, 'yet.'

'Sweetheart, you're a forty-year-old insurance telemarketer.'

'A very nice one,' Fleur added.

'I'm thirty-nine, and telemarketing is just the battery hen warehouse that I'm locked in now. In New York, I'll be top of the heap.'

'What an aspiration.' Adam rolled his eyes. 'Fleur, you can't leave me with this furball of idealism all by myself.'

'I've got to go,' she replied with a smile. 'And it won't matter if I'm at the bottom of some hill or heap, as long as it has a good view.'

The local township café sat in front of a lush green mountain, but Fleur wasn't looking at the view. Seized with panic, she was scrolling rental listings on her phone. Back in Sydney, Fleur had described the area she had envisioned living in as the 'meditative om' area. Since she last looked, 'om' had doubled in price and halved in rental listings. Even the African Drumming classes at the Community Hall looked expensive. After finely combing through employment opportunities, it became apparent that unless she had a forklift licence or a degree in sport and recreation, there was nothing to apply for.

Savings were down to double digits. Adam, eight months prior, had cut her credit card up. Fleur forgave the destruction, as she had cut up Adam's card at the same time. It had been a kind of suicide pact by two tragic consumerists one daiquiri-filled evening. Luckily for Adam, he had three other credit cards stashed away in his underwear drawer. Fleur hadn't organised a backup. Applying for another card wasn't doable until she had a job secured. Until the credit was no longer needed. Making matters worse, she had already overstayed her welcome at the home of the sister of a friend of a friend. At breakfast, there was mention of a relative coming to stay from out of town in two days' time. 'Sorry, Fleur, but we'll need the bed.'

Draining the rest of her latté, Fleur felt the milk turn in her stomach. Then the sound of the mosquito reappeared, buzzing about her right ear. With a shake of her head, she peered at the shire map on her phone like it was a crystal ball. She needed a solid next step. Or at least a reminder of what had brought her here. The university, with its own squad of landscape gardeners, was like a tropical oasis in a cluster of muffler shops and meat-platter raffles. Fully suited with hair tied back in a conservative bun, Fleur had shuffled her resume to anyone who would take it. At best, people nodded and smiled. At worst, their expression was as if she had just spat on the counter. Walking towards her car, she pulled her arm out as if stretching it, and dipped her nose towards her armpit, wondering if she smelt of 'city'.

While contemplating tobacco chewing as a career advancement strategy, Fleur visited the few available rentals. Ripped lino, burnt laminate, torn curtains, rusted, malfunctioning stove tops, and windows coated with a mixture of dust and grease. The air in every dwelling was musty with the faint odour of fried food. One unit was disturbed by death metal music played by a neighbour with Beethoven's ear.

Where well-heeled vegans lived was too expensive. The territory of carwash bikini girls was unthinkable. But there was a third area: Dairy country. Fleur's red Fiat travelled up hill, down dale, over serrated roads, around corners signposted at one hundred kilometres or more. Utility and multi-tonne trucks drove inches from her back bumper. Far from agreeable, the roads of rubble forced her to nod as she drove.

And then there it was. A dairy converted into a two-bedroom abode. Ten minutes away from ad nauseum panel-beaters, fifteen towards meditation marathons. The driveway was unkind, though Fleur foresaw the regular squashing of cane toads with her wheels to pave a smoother entry. A group of cows in a paddock behind the residence made noises as if they were missing their mufflers. But they made Fleur smile.

'Home converted from dairy' had a glossy magazine feel about it. The view from its hillside, through the tall trees, down to the lower paddock and rising back up to meet the sun was bona fide. But the house itself lacked skirting boards. Around most of the wall's edges was irregular honeycomb-style concreting. Fleur assumed that the pink walls in every room had to be done by a man, one with undercoat paint in abundance. Upon them was a bizarre pinboard effect of nails and screws. The previous tenant, armed ambidextrously with drill and hammer, must have had the strangest art hang in history. She shrugged to no one.

Striding into the real estate agency, she hocked up a good dose of high-density urban arrogance devised to outshine her unemployment status. After one call to Adam, who posed as referee and financial guarantor, Fleur left with a six-month lease. No additional skirting, painting of walls or extra nails permitted.

Here, you could get away from it all. Living in the middle of green, undulating paddocks, a person could find some peace and quiet. However, for Fleur, there was no peace in the quiet. The surrounding hills were majestic, but they blocked the mobile phone reception. And the local exchange had run out of internet lines.

'Run out of lines?' Fleur repeated into her phone. 'How is that even possible?' The call had already dropped out several times. She kept moving around the house, trying to find Mercury, the Greek god of communication. 'Didn't you guys see it coming?' Work was in completion, she was told, but it was nowhere near complete. 'It may take two more weeks, maybe more,' the disembodied voice replied. In a job-search flight-fright state, being contactable was paramount. Besides, she needed someone to talk to. She caught some range out by the highway. The Fiat soon became Fleur's social life, office, and therapy clinic. Except her sanity source had left the country.

'We're in Tahiti,' Adam explained on a voicemail message. 'It was an impromptu thing. Sydney hasn't been the same without you, so we left.'

At that point, Pete had seized the phone and added, 'Then in two weeks we go off to New York, New York, for almost a month.'

'So nice they named it twice, like Wagga Wagga,' Adam ended. Through the sarcasm, Fleur noticed glimmers of light-heartedness, and she could smell Adam's gin and tonic from her car. 'We'll keep in touch. Hoping you're doing okay over there, girl. There's something special lining up for you, I can feel it. There's a reason you went out to that part of the middle of nowhere.'

After playing the next message three times to catch it amongst the traffic noise surrounding her, Fleur learned that work on the telephone exchange had been delayed. It was going to take another two weeks before a possible connection. The sounds from a passing cattle truck drowned out the sounds of Fleur's fury.

Two days later, she was in range when she heard by voicemail about the accident. Adam had been scuba diving when a heart attack struck him. Before he died on the boat, he requested to be buried there in the deep and that Pete should continue with his New York plan.

'"*Make it there*," were his last words,' Pete sniffed.

She parked the car at the side of the freeway and digested the news. This involved pulling out the cleanskin Shiraz she just bought on special and drinking some hefty gulps before calling

Pete, who miraculously picked up. Where was he? What time was it for him? Did it matter?

'He was happy here, in Tahiti,' Pete said.

'He was. I heard it in his last message. Pete, are you coming home?'

'I want to, but I know I'll never leave if I do. Adam was right, I've got to keep going. People are going to think I don't care, but Adam's friends never really accepted me, being a telemarketer. Except you, Fleur. I'm grateful for that.'

'I'm grateful for our friendship, too, Pete.'

'It's scary though, going out on your own.'

'Tell me about it,' she said. 'Call me anytime, promise me. You can always come here. Wherever I end up,' she laughed, but the laugh had an unintended edge. Even the offer of talking on the phone felt futile, living out of range. She hung up, leaned her forehead on the steering wheel, and sobbed. Much to her shame, the practicalities of the situation came to mind. If she didn't get a job soon, the real estate agent would track Adam down as financial guarantor.

Fleur continued to visit employment agencies, shops, and offices with even greater feigned gusto than before. Each time, she copped the dreary words 'unskilled, no experience', 'over-qualified' or 'no, not at the moment'.

They held Adam's memorial service for friends and family in Sydney five days later, but the cost for Fleur to return was beyond reach. Instead, she looked outside at the rolling green hills and the sun that blanketed them. Spreading a picnic blanket on a patch of lawn in front of her new home, she settled down cross-legged and breathed. No plastic was required, in handset or credit card form. It was what came naturally. She tried to think of Adam, of Pete, of loss in general and of her own grief. But unfamiliar sounds around her, ones she hadn't noticed before, were catching her attention. The mooing was more multi-toned than taught in kindergarten. Birds shrieked manically before dive-bombing a dog in the distance. Fleur closed her eyes. In between nature's racket and the sound of her breath was silence. It didn't have a number, call waiting or voicemail, but she heard it. And, as Adam predicted, she discovered the reason she went out to that part of the middle of nowhere. It was the connection she had been looking for.

The unmistakable sound of a mosquito caught her attention. Fleur opened her eyes and saw it right in front of her. Far from being the size of Bloomingdale's, it wasn't any larger than mosquitoes found in the city. She smiled. And with one wave, it disappeared. Then her phone rang. Reception. The phone had reception. Fleur looked at her phone like it had sneezed. Then she realised it was Meera.

'Heard about your job tanking,' she said.

'The Sydney art world gossip machine is still running well, I see,' Fleur replied with a grimace.

'Your Instagram's been quiet. Got people asking questions.'

'Nice that they care.'

'I wouldn't go that far,' Meera said. 'Hey, I won a 12-month contract to start a mental health art therapy program focused on nature. It's a pilot, first of its kind.'

'Congratulations, Meera,' Fleur said, meaning it. It was comforting to hear some good news, even if it wasn't hers.

'That's brilliant.' She stared out over the landscape of trees and pastures as if she'd never seen them before. Well, she hadn't, not like this. They were—

'It's at the hospital out your way,' Meera said, interrupting Fleur's gaze. 'I need a full-time assistant. You'd be perfect.'

'What? Me?' Fleur sat up, alert. *Why would I be perfect?* But Meera had always seen things other people didn't. It's what artists do.

'Yes, you, Fleur. Are you in?'

'For the sake of mental health?' Then a kookaburra laughed, and three cows joined in. 'God yes, Meera, I am in.' Then a fly landed on her nose, and she laughed as she gently swatted it away. *Looks like we all are.*

THE CONDITIONAL GIFT*

[Egg-Free Sugar Cookie]

**The broken bits don't count*

'Spend each day as if it's your last,' Graham said to himself. He said it again, trying it out with an American accent, but it didn't make any difference. Graham's already sunken chest fell further inwards. The reality being, if this was going to be his last day, he wouldn't bother trying to make breakfast. Instead, he drew his dressing gown around him and took a deep breath from the doorway. Putting one aching leg in front of the other, he almost made it to the refrigerator when the doorbell rang.

'Bugger,' the old man said under his breath. 'Coming!' he yelled over it.

'It's only me,' the woman's voice from behind the door shrilled, ricocheting down the hallway.

'Hazard,' he muttered, making his way towards the front door with steps that were bird-like but with none of the bounce. Looking down, he cringed at the source of embarrassment below. Knitted purple slippers donned his shuffling feet. They were a recent gift from his daughter, arriving the same day the old, comfortable brown leather ones had mysteriously disappeared. 'The others were falling apart anyway, Dad,' she had said brightly.

'Too brightly,' Graham murmured down at their purpleness. 'Coming,' he repeated to the door. Once he finally met his destination, the next task felt like bomb diffusion. Graham focused on the door handle while his trembling knuckles knocked on the wooden panel.

'Come in,' the visitor laughed from the other side.

'Very funny,' Graham yelled back while trying to turn the knob. Hearing the 'click' brought tremendous relief. Once he opened the door, Graham could feel the cool morning air on his face. There, on his front step, were the predictabilities of the outside world.

'Morning, Graham,' his rosy-cheeked neighbour said, thrusting a full carton of a dozen eggs into his unsteady grip. 'Charlotte had a good run this morning,' she added.

'Pen...' Graham started. The visitor's name was Penny Hazard. Initially, he had tried avoiding her by not answering the door. But after a week of tenacious doorbell ringing, she contacted the police and reported a probable death. After the awkward experience of being found alive, Graham decided it was easier to accept the eggs and whatever came with them. Sometimes it was a bunch of parsley; sometimes it was an inquisition.

'How are you doing, Graham?'

Looking down, his shaking hands almost blurred the carton. 'Remember when I mentioned before about how I'm not supposed to have too much of this sort of thing?'

'Nonsense,' Hazard replied, 'eggs are excellent protein. You need your protein, Graham.'

'I'll have one with my toast,' he lied, 'which I've just put on.' Another lie. 'Better get back to the kitchen.'

'Okay,' she nodded efficiently. 'Well, make sure you get some fresh air sometime today, won't you?'

'Yes, Pen.'

At that, the woman pirouetted in her gumboots and headed towards the gate. Graham glared at her back before closing the door and negotiating his journey back to matters at hand.

While passing the lounge room doorway, he noticed Constantine sprawled across the orange settee. The sprawling sometimes made it hard for Graham to feel motivated. *'How was it,'* he mused, *'that cats could sleep so much but never look depressingly unappealing the way lethargic humans do?'* Constantine was a middle-aged grey tabby whose striped grey coat served no camouflage in his warm-toned surrounds. The animal obviously did not belong, yet appeared completely at ease in this unnatural place, particularly in times of stillness and silence.

Constantine's owner appreciated silence, but quietening those shaking hands was an impossible dream. While the cat mastered non-doing, or 'wu wei' as Graham's Taoist daughter-in-law called it, Graham did things. Beyond the enforced movement, he embarked on simple tasks and took forever.

When Graham was young, he found the second hand on his watch useful for timing laps in the swimming pool or on the running track. Then, in middle age, he forgot about seconds. Time became measured in minutes, hours, or days. In old age, the second hand had become significant again, but it was a tedious, demanding measurement of how little could be done, given limited resources.

Constantine looked back at Graham while stretching his front paws towards the television. 'Bumper-to-bumper tai chi in this place,' Graham replied before continuing the drawn-out shuffle towards the kitchen. When finally at the refrigerator, his aching knuckles knocked around the plastic handle, failing dismally at commanding the grip. Meanwhile, the second hand on the clock above the stove tapped like an impatient woman's heel. Seizing the handle with a rush of determination, the old door's suction pulled, then released. A yellow glow from the interior light shone on the smooth areas of Graham's furrowed complexion. Unaware of his golden blush, the old man steered the eggs on top of three other cartons previously delivered by Hazard.

Homemade marmalade, given by the wife of a friend six months before, remained on the door. 'I've been told to pass this on,' Roger had said with a heavy grin. The lid, covered by misleading pink floral fabric, required a gorilla's grip to open. Neither of the men liked marmalade anyway, so they cracked a couple of stubbies instead.

'You know how I'm not supposed to have too much of this sort of thing…' Graham chuckled at his beer.

'None of us are, Gray,' Roger replied with a shrug.

'Roger?'

'Yes, Graham?'

'Have you ever had a massage?'

The suggestion prompted the beer to shoot up Roger's nose. 'A what?' he asked, dabbing at his face with a handkerchief from his trouser pocket.

'Have you ever had a massage? A professional one, I mean.'

'A professional massage?' Roger pondered. 'I thought you might have been referring to the other kind…'

'No, but if I was younger,' he chuckled.

Roger snorted before settling back in his chair. 'To answer your question, my missus reckons they're all pretty suss, so the answer is no, I haven't. Why do you ask?'

Graham explained his dilemma. Trudi, the Taoist daughter-in-law, had just completed a therapeutic massage course. Her sights had locked onto Graham's aching body as a practise tool. Before there had been any laying on of hands, she had counselled Graham on his difficulty with 'receiving'.

'You are so giving, Graham,' she had said with trained earnestness. 'It's vital you learn how to receive if you want your health to improve.' She was all of twenty-seven when she explained her analysis to a man who may as well be the age of Moses. Graham had been proud that his son had scored such an attractive and vibrant wife, but the proposition of being massaged by her was, in his mind, ludicrous. And as far as Graham was concerned, a massage from anyone for his body would be like rearranging deck chairs on a vibrating Titanic. 'Plus,' he surmised to Roger, 'I'm not giving at all.'

'Too right, Gray, too right,' his friend nodded before taking another sip from his Tooheys.

Still standing in the refrigerator's cool air, the old man felt like all his organs had fallen from their designated positions and collected in his stomach. He was famished and nauseous at the same time. It was important to eat. Doctor's orders. 'Stop fussing and get on with it, man,' he coaxed himself. The trembling hands grasped a packet of sliced wholemeal bread, which was then thrown onto a nearby lime green laminate bench. Turning back, he addressed the butter. Picking it up, he banged the wrapped form between the shelves before placing it carefully, albeit dented, next to the bread. Butter trays with china lids hadn't fared well in this process.

'Piss easy,' he would have said once, when pissing was easy. Graham hovered momentarily over the tower of egg cartons, but it didn't take a prophet to see bits of eggshell in everything. He opted instead for a tall jar of blackberry jam given by someone. *'Who was it?'* he wondered. Someone had already cracked the lid open (*'By who?'*), the choice was sure-fire. Once the jar was on the bench, he closed the refrigerator door and straightened his back. 'Now for my next trick, the toaster.' Two slices of wholemeal flapped like flags above their destination. After three attempts, they were both in their respective slots. He pushed down the lever and, as the seconds ticked by, the bread slowly changed colour and became rigid.

During the toasting, Graham negotiated water into the cordless electric kettle. Most splashed around his hands, but just enough made it inside for a cuppa. With the push of a button, it began rumbling into life. He wiped his hands on a tea towel covered in kookaburras. It had been his wife's favourite. 'I'm a plain pattern man,' he murmured to himself. The thought came as a surprise and left as quickly when his stomach rumbled and turned. Mel used to make him porridge during the winter months. During their last summer together, she served up organic muesli.

'Where's the packet?' he had asked once.

'What do you want the packet for?'

'So I can eat it.'

'Graham,' she sighed.

'You're starving me deliberately, sending me to the grave early so you can live in luxury on your own.' Seconds came, and he was already in hindsight. It had been a stupid thing to say, and he knew what was coming next.

'Luxury!' Mel cried. 'What bleedin' luxury are you referring to now? This?' Her hands fluttered, then were open-palmed to the tiny kitchen like a magician prior to trickery.

'Well, after you've killed me, you'll find some other, richer fella, won't you?'

A ripple of a smile ran over Mel's face before starting on the dishes. *'Saved,'* Graham thought while gazing at his empty breakfast bowl. But in the older, more mature stage of hindsight, Graham realised just how far off the mark he was. Six weeks later, the oncology department delivered Mel's diagnosis. They both sat in the waiting room afterwards, trying to absorb the news. Waiting rooms were terrible places for thinking. Lit by cold fluorescent beams and surrounded by linoleum, year-old magazines and other people's problems, Graham eased Mel off the chair and took her home.

No one would have disputed Mel's tenacity. The pain had been going for weeks, and she hadn't said a word until that Monday. She had been a fighter alright. But this was more of a war than a fight. And it had begun without her. By the time they knew it was too late to join in. Though no one knew the timing of these things anymore.

Five weeks later, Mel passed away. A swift departure compared to the demise of others from the same department. But still torture. After the fuss of the funeral, anxiety, like froth, finally came to the surface. It couldn't have waited any longer. It was as if it had been holding its breath throughout Mel's deterioration. With Mel gone, it saw an opportunity for oxygen and lathered. After a night of unrelenting shaking and tears, Graham pulled himself together. Anxiety often led to soft crutches, yielding and pathetic. He had seen it happen to others. The new widower avoided bingeing from the following morning onwards; binge drinking, binge eating, binge thinking. The grieving process had been a careful one, Graham doing his best to tame it with the buckles and straps of his mind. Since that night of abandonment, he lived a precariously balanced life, never really recovering from the clutch of the middle ground.

Graham watched the kettle boil until the smoke caught his eye. Popping up the slices of blackened toast, he attempted to scrape the charcoal surface off one slice into the sink. Then the toast slipped from his grip and dropped into a small puddle of water left from filling the jug.

'Bugger, bugger, bugger,' Graham moaned through gritted teeth as he punched his fist into the sodden, blackened bread. His knuckles throbbed against the hard, unforgiving surfaces. Everything ached. Tears attempted to fight their way to the surface, but he wouldn't have it. Lips folding in, he drew a resolute breath through his nose and took out two more slices of wholemeal bread. On the way to the toaster, he contemplated various ways to destroy the kookaburra tea towel.

Despite the room's post-apocalyptic breakfast atmosphere, Constantine padded into the kitchen and crunched methodically on the remainder of his dry food from the night before. Like many cats, Constantine was a grazer. He never ate complete meals in one sitting. Graham, still hungry, dropped the bread on the bench and watched enviously from above. When the cat finished the bowl, he walked purposefully across to the other side of the room and began cleaning himself.

Graham's already aching legs shifted up to his pain threshold. Moving to the empty breakfast counter, he positioned himself on a stool and stared at the sheen of the green laminate before him. Graham had never formally meditated, but on that morning, he was close to it. While the clock above the stove continued to tick, accompanied by the baritone groans from his stomach, the old man held firm. After a few minutes, it came. The answer that had been with him the best part of his life, but he had been too afraid to utter it. 'Baked beans,' he announced to the empty space. 'I've always wanted baked beans on toast for breakfast.'

At that moment, Graham's heart lifted, then just as soon gave way. Pain shot up the right-hand side of his body, and his head hit the laminate with the weight of a concerned friend's casserole. None of this stopped his lips from moving to taste the baked beans conjured delectably in his mind. Within seconds - though by now Graham wasn't counting - the baked beans were gone. His shoulders sagged, the rest of his body followed, and breath left his lungs for good. Graham's eyes, however, remained open, staring out impassively. The expression was not new. It had been the same every time he had been forced to receive an unwanted gift.

A GiRL'S GUiDE TO FiRE

[Burnt Butter & Toffee Cookie]

She said nothing when the light globe dropped out of her hand. Teetering on a tower of art books on a wooden box on a chair, Carla was concentrating on poise. The globe, strapped into the seat of gravity, had quite a journey to the floorboards below. A whole phrase of colourful blasphemy could have been yelled in that time if she had felt steady enough. Instead, she heard a string of expletives from outside. Then the ladder flew past the window.

Carla turned her gaze from the window to the globe below. Already blown, its body appeared intact, but was rolling back and forth as if in pain. Returning her attention to the matter at hand, she asked herself, *how many glass artists does it take to change a light bulb?* The new globe clicked into place. *None,* she replied, *because they didn't get the funding.* Carla made a mental note to tell it to Howard sometime. He would laugh and add, 'Except you, my little go-getter.' Not on that day, however. She could hear Howard moaning, 'Bloody hell,' from what was possibly the back garden. Acoustics were strange in the place. The August winds carried Howard's aggravations, moving them around corners as if they were searching for her.

When the bulb felt secure, Carla glanced at her hands. They looked middle-aged. This was because she worked with her hands. And because she was almost middle-aged. *Thirty-eight,* she mused with no great pang of loss. While failing at maths at twelve, Carla had resolved that life was to improve as she grew older. It had to. Nothing could be worse than long division.

Jumping down, just missing the old globe, Carla looked up while flicking the switch. *And then there was light*, she nodded before noticing the clock. It was already eight-thirty. While making her way down the hall, Carla spotted Howard's cropped brown hair through the back windows. Their house, a weatherboard Queenslander on stilts designed for capturing breezes of the Sunshine Coast's sub-tropical climes. It had a view of the sea, though when they last went to the beach was hard to recall. The height of the house often enabled Carla to feel she was above life's frustrations. Often, but not always.

Howard's swearing began with small, punctuated phrases. Punches of words. 'Bloody hell' - two words and three-syllables - didn't demand a response. He took the Lord's name in vain occasionally. But as Howard was an atheist, he didn't seem to get much mileage out of it. When the swearing settled into place, like it wasn't going to leave for a while, one-syllable words ending in 't' or 'k' pitched forth. That was when Carla started feeling her way towards him, wherever he was.

But it seemed she either ventured out too soon or not soon enough. After trying to understand what Howard's problem was, she would then be fool enough to make suggestions. There were attempts at moaning along with him, but that just created a silence of untenable fury. When she suggested taking a break, Howard looked like he could easily snap her in two. Physical violence only happened to inanimate objects, like hardware tools with expired guarantees. While changing the light globe, Carla knew what was coming and decided upon a fresh approach.

She was grabbing her keys and handbag as Howard's one-syllable word hit the air with its hardened end. From the hallway, Carla could see him around the side of the house, mangling an ill-fitting fly screen into a complex moth-like form. Then his head and the fly screen both dropped from view. She turned and saw Howard again, but this time in a framed photograph by the front door. She hesitated at it, at them during their first year together. Howard had longer hair then, with blonde streaks from the sun. He was working on the boats around that time, passionate about research. *Passionate but also relaxed,* Carla noted, peering closer at the two figures as if into a microscope. *We both looked so relaxed.*

'Where are you going?' Howard yelled as she closed the front door behind her. He was standing near the compost bin, two metres from the carport. The wind was picking up. She pulled her hair away from her face before walking down the steps towards the driveway.

'To the studio, I'm already late,' she yelled back. Howard's sunglasses were off. There was no point in having them on when glare was coming from the eyes.

'Fine.' He slammed the ladder against the house only to watch the windowpane crack across a corner. He threw the ladder back to the ground as if in punishment, then Howard stormed off down the side of the house. His disappearance meant nothing. As far as Carla was concerned, he had been gone all morning. Who this other man was, she couldn't be sure, but he was becoming familiar.

Carla slipped into the driver's seat and turned on the ignition. Bach blasted through the speakers and through her body, prompting a scramble for the volume control. With *Brandenburg Concerto Number Three* almost mute, she pulled out of the driveway. The street was peaceful enough. Its jacaranda branches bent to one side, showing the wind was now at her back.

The August wind period was a Queensland meteorological ritual that ushered in the oppressive hot spring months. The hot spring months were the forerunners to the monsoonal rains. 'Then,' Janet said, 'we get some decent weather.'

'Let's hope so,' Carla replied while sweating in front of the furnace. You would think the furnace was the hottest spot in the studio. But the glory hole gave the furnace a run for its money. The furnace melted the raw ingredients. Sand, limestone, soda and potash. The glory hole served as a second furnace, reheating the glass so it didn't crack from cooling too quickly while being worked.

A government department had ordered six large glass bowls for an award ceremony. Jeremy, the apprentice, looked at the government brief, then threw the pages back on the desk. 'I know what else those funding-sucking politicians could do with these bowls.'

'Best keep the glass hot on the blow-pipe for that,' Graham replied, his balding head shining from the fluorescent lights above.

'As manager of this workshop,' Carla announced with a suppressed smile, 'I must remind you that this kind of job is now our bread and butter.'

Jeremy added, 'Sand-wiches.'

Carla took a hollow piece of steel pipe and rotated it in the molten glass, as if gathering honey onto a spoon. 'Remind me, Janet, when does Queensland's good weather start? It does start sometime, right?'

Janet looked up, pulling her hair back from her perspiring face, 'It gets better. About April, maybe May.' Carla then walked across to a metal-topped bench. Janet blew the molten blob of glass into a round shape. Together, they gathered and rolled the glass.

'Next April,' Carla mused. 'Sounds like quite a wait.'

'Just as well you don't have children or pets. The August winds drive them mad,' Janet replied. 'Then again,' she chuckled, 'you have Howard, don't you?'

Janet was being playful, but her comment stung like a thousand tiny sparks across Carla's face. Camouflaged by furnace heating, she worked around the glory hole and allowed her imagination to wander. Before too long, she was sinking into a cool sunlit pool. In her mind, she was wearing swimming goggles rather than workshop safety ones. Plunging deep into the fresh pool, she turned to gaze up at the kaleidoscope of light mixing with the lazy rippling surface. It was more a memory than anything, something done a thousand times as a child over summer holidays. While other children were splashing each other and playing games, Carla was swimming down, then turning to look up at the surface light, staying under the water for as long as her tiny lungs would allow. And at that moment the light and the water were all. There wasn't anything else.

Turning away from the glory hole, Carla almost hit Graham and dropped the pipe. With a dexterous movement, Janet caught it just before the glass hit the floor.

'Sorry, Graham,' Carla rushed, 'didn't see you there.'

'I wasn't expecting you to go that way.'

'Me neither,' she replied. 'I lost my concentration. Thanks for the save, Janet.'

'No problem.'

Janet blew the pipe, then rolled it back and forth across the arms of the bench while Carla shaped the glass using a hardwood paddle and jack. From time to time they returned the pipe to the glory hole for reheating. When complete, Graham cracked off the bowl from the blowpipe with the touch of a cold pincher and placed it into an annealing oven to cool down slowly. Jeremy was supposed to check the timing, but he was on the phone laughing with an unreliable supplier.

Carla clicked on the timer and took a swig from her litre water bottle. She imagined somebody, perhaps someone as young and foolish as Jeremy, seizing the bottle out of her hands and pouring the entire contents over her head. The cold liquid would crawl down her body agonisingly slowly before coming to rest at her feet. And then she could evaporate completely.

Janet was either forgetful or prophetic. Howard and Carla had pets, two goldfish called Crumbed and Battered. But something happened a week later. Noticing that Crumbed and Battered weren't their perky selves, Howard had fiddled with the filter for hours – swearing, of course – unable to find a problem. He changed the water over, scrubbed away any remnant of algae and checked the pH, the carbonates and temperature. But the next morning, Howard found Crumbed and Battered belly up on the surface like a couple of miniature floaties.

Just before the funeral service, Howard moaned about being a marine biologist 'for almost twenty years' who couldn't keep two goldfish alive. Carla squatted with him in the back garden, looking at the two little gravesites prepared next to the frangipani tree. The branches were bending from the wind, as if they were bowing mourners in attendance. 'Three years is a pretty good innings,' she offered over the rustling of the trees and shrubs around them.

'They deserved longer.' Howard replied.

Her hand reached to touch his. 'You did everything you could.'

A shadow of a grin flickered in Howard's profile. Carla had always suspected that people were their own mirrors, walking opposites. It depended on the way the light hit as to which side was going to show.

'They wouldn't have been much good as long-term family members anyway,' he replied. 'No concentration span, hopeless at washing dishes.'

'Rubbish on that front, definitely,' Carla nodded, pulling her hair from her face against the breeze.

The ceremony was a selected reading from Moby Dick and a minute of silence. Even the wind seemed to settle into the moment. Then Howard looked at his watch. 'I'd better get moving, the meeting is in twenty minutes. They want to formalise the new position, introduce me to staff, tour the site...'

'It all sounds very important.' She almost added, 'Your mother will be proud.'

Howard's mother was so delighted to hear about her son's new job that she threw a Sunday afternoon party to celebrate it. The job had been unexpected for everyone, in the industry as well as Howard's family.

Fed up with losing tourism dollars to the Gold Coast's brassy Water World and associated plastic-coated theme parks, Queensland's Sunshine Coast councils made an unprecedented and highly confidential move of fraternity. They combined certain 'yet to be allocated' funds for a spectacular yet tasteful aquarium, an aquarium that would put their water back on the map. Howard had been head-hunted for the Aquarium's marine logistics manager, earning payroll security, superannuation and an executive car.

'Now *this* is a great opportunity,' Howard's father would have said if he was still above ground. But he wasn't, and Howard was standing, alive and well and trapped in his mother's lounge room next to the buffet table. As always, the air-conditioning was powered at full throttle. The body heat of sixteen relatives jammed in that tiny, doilied room failed to compete with it. Carla stood next to Howard, shivering while listening to Grandma Hettie outline her international cricket predictions for the forthcoming season. While Carla nodded in all the right places, she was listening to Howard's dead father whispering into his son's ear, 'This is what I've been talking to you about, Howie. The Ladder of Success.'

While Mr Taylor was alive, the rules of The Ladder of Success had been recited at the family dinner table more often than Grace. Howard had tried to explain it the night Carla was to meet his parents for the first time. Mr Taylor had been big in industrial refrigeration, and so demonstrated a clear example of how this ascending path with rungs worked. There had never been an expectation for Howard to follow his father's footsteps into the bitter climes of refrigeration, just somewhere in the vicinity of corporate management.

To Mr Taylor's surprise, Howard discovered the beach. Beach holidays had never featured in the Taylor holiday schedule. Sunburn had been a major concern. So when Howard chose to hang from the threads of contracted government aquatic projects, Mr Taylor spent most of the time shaking his head with a mixture of disapproval and bewilderment.

Recent years had seen change, however. Howard's skills

and experience had accumulated into 'management material'. In inescapable increments, Howard's time was spent more often behind the office desk than swaying on watercraft. Mr Taylor observed this development from the island that was his deathbed. Both father and son seemed to drain of colour simultaneously. The old man's shaking head ground to a halt on the puffed-up hospital pillow while a smile formed on his pale lips. Two months later, the smile dropped a little. and the eyes stopped watching. That had been four years ago.

'Everything's going your way, Howie,' Carla heard Uncle Eric yell over the rumble of Mrs Taylor's air conditioning. He then slapped his nephew on the back so hard the mini quiche almost regurgitated.

'Howard, I prefer Howard.'

'But your Dad always called you Howie...'

'Yes, and he's dead now.' The joke fell flat on Uncle Eric, who looked like he'd just swallowed a bad Devil on Horseback. However, it didn't stop the man from collecting three more from the platter before shimmying towards Aunt Rhoda in the corner. Carla smiled over her shoulder in a show of support while Grandma Hettie paused for a tuna tartlet. The old woman then spotted her great-grandson who was certain to be a more receptive sports conversationalist.

'Are you alright?' Carla asked Howard through chattering teeth.

'Yes, but you're freezing,' he yelled over the air-conditioning. 'I'll go get your green cardigan from the car.'

'My cardigan! I forgot to bring it.'

'I remembered,' he spoke loudly into her ear before kissing her cheek. 'You always forget about the suburban Ice Age.'

'My hero,' Carla cried as he got his keys out from his pocket and planned the best route to the front door. At that point, the air conditioning was roaring to a crescendo. She watched Howard make his move. The air conditioner belched. The power blacked out and the room became as silent as the grave just as Carla shouted, 'Please take me with you!'

'There's a saying,' Howard said, rising from the tiny gravesites of Crumbed and Battered. 'When everything is coming your way, it means you're on the wrong side of the road.'

'What's on your mind?' she asked.

'I don't know,' he moaned, brushing grass off the knees of his suit. 'This job, it's a great opportunity.'

'I suppose it is,' Carla nodded. 'A great opportunity for what exactly? What do you want out of this?'

'Well, it's a promotion, isn't it?'

'The Ladder of Success, you mean?'

'You can laugh, but it is more money,' he replied. 'More money means we pay off the mortgage faster and I can inject something into the workshop now that the funding...'

'Oh no, don't make this about me,' Carla threw up her hands. 'The workshop will be fine.' Howard looked at her sideways. 'And no,' she added, 'I don't mind going back to teaching if I have to.'

'What about the kids?' he asked.

'We don't have any kids. Crumbed and Battered are, as you can see, dearly departed.'

'We can afford that IVF program now.'

'What?' she asked, incredulous.

'I thought you would embrace the chance for a test-tube baby.'

'Why?' While panic started up in her stomach, her mind

commenced fast work on the puzzle. Ladder of Success. Got the car, got the house, got the job. Children?

'Well, for a start, they make test tubes out of glass…' he said.

'Howard, don't joke about this.' Children are precious. Not mini-beakers held over a Bunsen burner. 'Ten years ago, we got the results, shrugged our shoulders and got on with things. We never even discussed IVF.'

'Because we didn't have the money.'

'And because you weren't all that keen in the first place,' she replied. 'Are you saying that you now want to have a child?' Carla felt like she had morning sickness already.

Howard gazed down at the small graves. 'I don't know.'

'Well, let me know when you do.' Carla wanted to slap him hard on the back just like Uncle Eric. 'And, by the way, I'm turning forty in two years.' At that, she showed him her watch.

'Christ, I'm late for the meeting.' Howard left sprinting.

It was dark by the time he returned home. 'It's going to be the biggest aquarium in the southern hemisphere,' Howard recounted while Carla perched on her drawing board stool. They sat together in the office-storage room, drinking beer. Overhead spotlights illuminated the array of coloured glass vases, bowls, glasses and sculptural pieces that lined the walls. The room at night reminded them both of scuba diving in tropical coral reef areas. The colours almost floated.

'But we already know it's going to be the biggest aquarium in the southern hemisphere,' Carla replied. 'They used that line to hook you in. No pun intended.'

'But I kept hearing it like some surreal recorded message. I heard it from the recruitment officer. Then I heard it from the recruitment manager, then the chief executive officer, then the marketing and development officer. While attending a Board of Management meeting for a brief introduction, they all said, "It's going to be the biggest aquarium in the southern hemisphere," practically in unison with the verve of a Wagnerian chorus. I'm wondering if they put something in the coffee.'

'What if it's in the water?' Carla laughed. 'Those poor fish.'

'Hey, guess what?'

'What?'

'The CEO thought you might like to do some glass art for the kiosk.'

'A kiosk?' she laughed, beer almost finding its way back up through her nose. 'Do they still have those? I thought they died along with bikinied beauty queens.'

'What?' Howard asked aghast. 'Bikinied beauty queens are dead?'

'Maybe it's just the way I prefer to see the world…'

'Well, apparently, the world still has kiosks. At least they do in the largest aquarium in the southern hemisphere.'

'I don't mind kiosks,' she said. 'In fact, I think it's brilliantly retro of them.' 'Probably,' Howard smiled. 'Sorry about earlier, bringing up the IVF thing at the funeral. It wasn't the best timing.'

'There's nothing wrong with discussing it, I was just unprepared.'

'Well, what do you think?'

Carla sipped from her bottle before replying. 'This may sound a little naff,' she curbed, 'but I just want you to be happy.'

'So, you think I'll be happy if we have a child?'

'No, I don't.' She slipped off the stool, unsure where she was going.

'Why?' he asked. 'And what about you being happy?'

'I'd be a lot happier if you were happier.'

'But having a family would be great though, wouldn't it?' Howard said while scratching the label of the bottle.

'With your temper?' she asked quietly.

'My temper?' Howard's eyes widened while his body rose from the chair to meet her.

Carla automatically backed away, and her elbow knocked into a shelf. Howard caught the red vase, but the other two, a black and a purple one, smashed on the floor. The tiny shards looked like shrapnel and may as well have been embedded in her skin. She cried out, but couldn't form a word from it, and found herself squatting with her hands over her head.

'*My* temper? How about *your* clumsy…' Howard started. 'I'll go get the dustpan and broom, considering you're just going to sit there.'

Being accident-prone was not a quality valued in a glass artist. In the past, Carla had been well-coordinated. But the dropping and knocking of objects was becoming familiar and she, with every incident, increasingly fragile.

With the aid of private investors, the aquarium kiosk job became a glass commission worth half a million dollars. It involved an enormous café on ground level - enticing large families to eat cumbersome quantities - and a fine dining restaurant on the upper level, targeting couples and business groups who would be eating small portions at cumbersome prices. Next to the restaurant were conference and seminar rooms equipped with the latest audio-visual presentation technology. All areas were fully air-conditioned.

The décor brief was 'avoid placing aquariums in view of the diners.' Apparently, it was too obvious a design and, as the menu was predominantly seafood, the effect often led to vegetarianism. Carla suggested feature walls of glass reeds up to seven-foot high in various greens, blues and yellows, lit with slow-muting timers that gave the impression of being underwater. It was colourful without being gaudy, contemporary without being cold and suggested movement without promoting seasickness. Both the board and hospitality department loved the concept, particularly when Carla explained it would be the largest kiosk glass commission in the southern hemisphere.

There had been no more talk of children since the vases broke. There hadn't been much talk at all. Carla and Howard were working for the same organisation but only saw each other through half-opened eyes before tumbling into sleep or struggling to wake up. Carla did notice Howard wasn't losing colour anymore. He was becoming semi-transparent.

'You guys need to get away after the aquarium opens,' Janet said over a chicken tandoori pizza slice. It had become the standard workshop dinner, either wood-fired pizza or Thai takeaway. The team had reserved sushi for the final night of installation.

Carla crunched on her crust. 'Howard will have to stay a while for teething problems.'

'Okay,' Janet said, 'how about we go to Club Med together, and when Howard's ready to join you, I'll come back?'

'Now that's a plan,' Carla chuckled. 'Hey, where's Graham?'

'In the toilet, meditating.'

Jeremy was in the office on the phone with his girlfriend, pizza slice in hand. The telephone had been their relationship for the past two months. From the look on his face, the girl wasn't the patient kind.

'If nothing else,' Carla mused while taking another slice, 'we're all learning a lot about each other through this job.'

'Let's not forget the half mil.'

'I'll try not to.'

'Seriously, what about the Club Med idea?'

'Great offer, but I love Howard.'

'You're hilarious,' Janet said, moving towards a slice of capricciosa. After that, they ate in silence, listening to Jeremy lose tolerance while Graham regained it.

'I wonder if they'll ever find out we used bottles from the dump for half these reeds.'

'Jeremy,' Janet hissed. 'It's the final night of this godforsaken installation. Do you want to stuff it up now?'

'But no one's here,' he whined. He was also eyeing the sushi platter reserved for later.

'Only the marine logistics manager is here, but I won't tell,' Howard replied from across the room. 'The acoustics are pretty noisy, how are people supposed to hear their loved ones crack lobster legs in this place?'

'Are you suggesting we put carpet tiles on the walls instead?' Carla asked while walking towards him. His complexion was like eggshell against the dark fabric of his suit. The new and expensive suit, the suit she had never seen before. *Who did he buy it with,* she wondered, remembering the last time they bought a suit. Howard was hopeless. She had to guide him through the entire process. Now he looked elegant and awful at the same time.

'Only if the carpeting costs half a million dollars, they are very strict with budgeting here.' Howard kissed Carla on the cheek. 'It looks great, you should be very proud.'

'Thanks, how are you going?'

'Fine, I guess,' he replied. 'There are always mistakes, but we fix them.'

'Sounds like it's all in hand then.'

'Yep,' Howard sighed. 'Well, better not disturb.'

'You're going already?'

'There's a water displacement thing I have to sort out.'

'So that's it?'

'What?'

'You come in here, pat me on the head…'

'I kissed you.'

'On the cheek, it's the same thing.' The auditory effects of the space made Carla's disturbed voice almost operatic. 'You come in here, after all these weeks…..'

'You've never visited me at my office. Not once.'

'God knows I've tried, but I can't get past all the security and your PA keeps blocking my calls.'

'I *never* told her to do that –'

'Then you tell me "good job" before I even get to light it for you. And you're wearing that…that new suit I've never seen before.'

'You like it?'

'I loathe it.'

'It's Armani.'

'It's foreign.'

'You are a "Made In Australia" representative now?'

'I mean it's foreign to *me*.' Carla had lowered her voice. The workshop team heard every word, but Jeremy's attention was split between the argument and the untouched food.

'What's your problem, Carla?'

'Who did you buy that suit with?'

'I can buy a suit on my own.'

Carla could see how the indignant pale face betrayed him. She could see right through it. 'Is this how you fix things, Howard? You don't throw things around anymore. You just cover them up instead?'

'Look, I know you're tired…'

'Damn right, I am.' Fury possessed Carla. She felt her body striding across the room. She watched herself pick up a restaurant chair and throw it. Right at the installation.

Never had faux-bentwood flown so swiftly. Howard cast himself in front of it, tipping the end of a leg, but the chair kept hurtling with great velocity towards the tranquil reeds. Janet leapt high and sideways like an athletic outfielder, while Graham and Jeremy gasped in horror. Janet's hands, splayed like two large pink starfish, blocked the chair and saved what had become of old used bottles.

'Not fond of the seating, then?' Howard asked, still gathering breath. 'Personally, I think the acoustics are the real problem.' The room remained quiet. 'So what was that exactly?'

With everything inside spent, Carla's knees gave way. She fell to the floor, just missing the chair she had thrown. Janet knelt down, collecting Carla up and holding her as if she had just been glued together.

Howard crouched down with concern, but his head

instinctively shook with disapproval and bemusement as his father's had once done. 'Aren't you just hurting yourself, trying to break something you've worked so hard on?'

Carla raised her face to his. Her eyes had never been more reflective. Cheeks flushed with colour, Howard stopped shaking his head. Then the air-conditioning switched to a new cycle.

The rental boat rocked like a metronome for slow learners. The sky had been reasonably clear all morning. Carla and Howard drank some more water before zipping up their wetsuits.

'Janet offered to come to Club Med with me while you finished.'

'That Club Med tart,' Carla replied, grinning. 'Just as well the entrance installation didn't take as long as the kiosk.'

'And yet it cost the aquarium more,' Howard deliberated. 'You really are becoming quite the businesswoman.'

'Well, they could afford it. They don't have to pay your fat wage anymore.'

'They are still looking for someone else to take over the position.'

'But you're irreplaceable, didn't they know that?'

'Not when they accepted my resignation.' Howard looked out over the water, then turned to Carla. 'Are you okay?'

'Yes, I think so,' she replied, clipping on her oxygen tank. 'Are you?'

'Well, I'm still a little shocked that the test tubes didn't deliver. I was getting used to the idea of becoming a Dad, you know?'

Carla nodded, 'Me too.'

'Yeah, I always thought you'd make a great dad. Better than me.'

'Shut up, you big blouse,' she said, laughing, while checking her pressure gauge. Then Carla stopped and looked at him. 'What needs your nurturing,' she said, 'is what's under this water.'

'And you,' he said.

'All of us,' she said, standing up. 'Last one to the bottom is a rotten sea cucumber.' After popping the regulator in her mouth, she saw Howard's fins were already disappearing into the ocean. Even though his head was just below the surface, Carla could tell he was already down there. She hurried to join him. In just a few moments, they would both be looking up from the bottom, watching patterns of light shift through the water. Where there was nothing else.

THE HiDDEN PEOPLE

[Cream-Filled Chocolate Cookie]

'We all know it, Jo. You're a stubby short of a six pack,' Nora declared to her audience after jumping on a bar stool, then the bar itself. All single-handed. Nora's beer was coming with her. Even on *terra firma* she was hard to miss. Nora's braided hair, the colour of a fresh match head, was twisted into the outline of Mickey Mouse ears. Her voice and hair had quickly grabbed the attention of Jo's supporters, plus everyone else in the place. Packed bodies combined with Sydney's humidity made for a sticky jam, but the happy hum that had started back at the gallery was growing here. Once at Oxford Street's Brighton Bar, voices became louder as postures relaxed. Wallets finally began to surface, not for art but for alcohol. Then Nora started.

'Jo was spending so much time alone in that studio, staring at the canvas, and practically inhaling those instant noodles.' Nora's eyes were wide. She could have been telling a ghost story next to a campfire. 'All acts of a madwoman,' she added with red braided ears flapping. Jo stood near to the fire extinguisher. Her tired but large blue eyes hid under a mop of bog-standard brown hair. At least her Noah had waited until after the opening to launch her speech. 'One vodka-driven evening two months ago, things had started to look up,' Nora continued. 'Jo painted an abstract work using acrylic, much of it applied by the next-door neighbour's Persian cat, Muffin...'

The Muffin collaboration didn't feature in the exhibition that night. Jo's sober paintings were known to be photorealist, the style that inevitably raises the comment, 'It looks just like a photo, *really*' from even the most astute art critics. But talent is subject to fashion. Followers have a tendency to vacillate. Ten years earlier, computer-generated art was considered 'contemporary chic' and, much like rap music, had hung on longer than expected. Artists with brushes, particularly those who could paint like a photograph, had been considered quaint for a decade. But the backlash finally flung back, and Jo's work became sought after. Her prices rose and a solo exhibition was scheduled. *The Sydney Morning Herald* ran a two-page feature in their arts section. Then the national media picked up the scent and ran.

However, Jo's success largely depended on those who could afford to pay for a one-by-two metre painting that looked like a photograph of something real. Each meticulous painting demanded at least six weeks to complete. Time had become as valuable as the technique itself. Collectors began to revel in describing to friends and colleagues how long it took to produce their new purchase. No sweat shops, just one hand and a lot of perspiration.

But technology did not elude Jo's work completely. The paintings generally depicted a solitary figure in a room, sitting at a computer or in front of a television, faces lit by the artificial glow. The subject never looked at the screen, but was instead absorbed with an object in hand, or simply gazing nowhere with unexplained thoughts.

Wearing his best shirt, Jo's father worked his way towards her through the throng of exhibition guests. He had already seen the paintings hanging earlier that day, knowing he could then make a brief appearance at the opening. He was more of a rugby bloke. Not that he didn't appreciate Jo's hard work and extraordinary technique.

'They look just like photos. Incredible,' he had said, shaking his head, as he always did. The man was also like a boat without a rudder with Jo's mum no longer around. They were both still getting used to that. When he finally made it to his daughter that evening, he cupped his hand around her cheek with affection, kissed her other cheek and said, 'Well done, love,' before making his way to the door and retreating to the suburbs. Her mother would have said the same as her father. But she would have stayed until the end, moving on to the pub with her friends.

Dignified buyers nodded to Jo with quiet but absolute acknowledgement of a deal well done, then defaulted to their respective restaurant bookings. Gallery director, Owen Marks, was feeling a little more energetic. Despite his seventy years and associated arthritic obstacles, he possessed the charm of Anthony Hopkins and the sexual ambition of James Bond. That is, if Bond was gay. Owen slipped out of the gallery alone to seek out something less refined and younger at Club Wet.

At the bar, Jo watched her life being interpreted by Nora while the right side of her ribcage was being crushed by the bar's wedge. She wondered why she was having trouble feeling anything, except her aching wrist from holding a paintbrush for too long.

'You have always been crazy,' Nora thrust her Great Northern lager over the crowd towards Jo, 'but that's why I love you. I couldn't ask for a better friend.' She hesitated for a few seconds. The audience waited. 'Okay, I *could* ask for a better friend. One that doesn't need to be bound, gagged and dragged up Oxford Street to come out drinking. Anyway, here you are. All ten major works sold on opening night,' the crowd ruptured in applause. 'Okay…okay,' Nora continued, flapping her hand at her audience, 'Let's raise our glasses. To a sell-out show by the one who never sold out.' Even the bar staff cheered. Elbows knocked about happily in the toast, and drinks spilled like time-patterned surges from fountains. Jo nodded in thanks while congratulatory pats slapped about her shoulders. She focused on feeling them. Kalimba, Owen's gallery assistant, appeared next to her and nudged a congratulations with her body and a grin. The only problem with Kalimba being Owen's gallery assistant is that she was generally more striking than the art. Tall, dark-skinned of Somalian heritage with long dreadlocks, eyes moved with her. But she used whatever she had to her advantage, selling art with a clairvoyant-like understanding of buyers and catching whatever Owen dropped. Kalimba was gallery gold.

The bar was ruckus noisy, so Kalimba leaned in towards Jo's ear and shared the simple words, 'This is your time.' And at that moment Jo's face let go of its multitude of tiny muscles, previously hooked up into a contrived smile. The same sort of smile that often came uninvited when squinting hard at her work, looking for error. But now, relaxation was beginning its journey through her body. A blissful tingling came as her shoulders sagged. A sigh escaped her lips in respite. A woman standing on the other side of her asked if something was wrong.

***

This is my time, Jo told herself a week later. She was walking towards the Owen Marks Gallery, mentally gearing up for a meeting with Timothy Banks, a high-profile thirty-something architect from the city. He hadn't visited the gallery yet.

'Timothy saw your images on the website,' Kalimba explained on the phone.

'You can't appreciate the detail on the site,' Jo exasperated. 'He wouldn't feel the dimension, the impact.'

'Well, he felt something,' she said. 'And, according to Owen, it's significant.'

It turned out that Timothy Banks felt a few things, namely size, budget and a gallery reputation. He wanted to commission a large painting, three times the size Jo usually braved. It would be for the foyer of a new city development called Edifice. Owen Marks chose to pronounce the development 'Edifarce'.

Jo and Timothy were seated in the office. Nearby, Kalimba was cleaning out some files from a cabinet, one eye on the security monitor. The gallery was still empty. Timothy was distracted by the vision of Kalimba while Jo stared at her hands. Their coffees sat cooling on Owen's desk before them. The white glossy desk was minimalist in design, but Owen had betrayed the designer's dreams by piling it with clutter, including art magazines, newspapers, finance folders, USB sticks, a book on cats, old camera equipment and a small, unfired clay sculpture of a wonky kangaroo.

'A gift from his niece,' Kalimba explained as she made space for the coffees.

Owen was supposed to be there to guide Jo's first corporate commission, but no one could trace the man. 'He's getting forgetful,' Kalimba had whispered when Jo walked into the gallery.

'Timeline's a little tight,' Timothy said after sipping his soy latté and turning his attention back to Jo. 'We've got about three weeks.'

'Three weeks?' Jo choked. 'It's not possible.' She was already pining for a break from painting, for her wrist if nothing else. The financial profit from the show had been considerable, but most of the money was already earmarked for accumulated debts. Picasso had his Blue Period. Jo had her Unfashionable Period.

'Maybe you already have something back at the studio?' Timothy asked.

'My largest paintings are all here. I only have small studies left.'

Timothy thought for a moment. 'Hey, what if we clustered all the studies into one work?'

'You mean hang them collectively?'

'As one,' Timothy replied enthusiastically, 'like a grid. Then all you have to do is paint a huge shadowy outline of a figure over the lot of them. That'll tie it all together.'

Jo reeled back speechless while Owen Marks strode into the office all smiles. 'Sorry I'm late, folks. Bugger of a time getting a…never mind.' Kalimba walked back out to attend the gallery desk. Changing of the guard. Meanwhile, Timothy briefed Owen on the conversation to date. Jo sat in her chair, silently yearning for anti-inflammatories and the opportunity to curl up in a ball in bed. 'I hear what you're saying, my boy,' the gallery director groaned as he sat down, needing anti-inflammatories of his own. 'But that's just not going to fly. You're dealing with photo-realism, not post-modernist cut-outs. Photo-realism takes time, but it's worth the wait. Jo had a sell-out show opening night. Haven't had that since the early nineties.'

'I have deadlines, Owen. The kind that emphasises the "dead" part.'

'Don't tell me the building is finished and ready for a foyer masterpiece.'

'Almost.'

'I still see cranes out there at Edifarce, Timothy,' Owen said, waving his arm towards the street. 'Cranes.'

'Edifice,' Timothy corrected, clearly annoyed. 'They're just about finished up top. The interior is on schedule.'

Owen looked slyly at the architect before turning to Jo. 'What do you need time-wise, dear?'

'Thirteen weeks minimum,' she replied, 'after the concept is accepted.'

'Thirteen weeks?' Timothy gasped.

'Have a problem with the number thirteen, Timothy?' Owen chuckled. 'What's that thing called where an architect decides against having a thirteenth floor?'

'Triskaidekaphobia,' Timothy replied glumly, like someone with chronic fatigue who is still able to roll myalgic encephalomyelitis off the tongue.

'Will Edifarce have a thirteenth floor?'

'It's called Edifice, Owen. And no, we haven't decided yet.'

'You haven't decided on how many floors you're having and yet you attempt to pressure this magnificent artist into...'

'We know how many floors we're having, just not what to call them.'

And so it went. Ultimately, they agreed on a general concept and a ten-week term for painting, given no changes will be made by Timothy's firm after final concept approval. Jo wondered why Owen didn't bat for the thirteen she needed.

Owen signed the contract first. The one Kalimba had prepared based on discussions to date. Timeframes were filled in with ballpoint. Jo hovered the pen over the contract, apprehensive about the timeline. She rubbed her aching wrist while staring at Owen. He winked back and nodded towards the paper. Timothy took the pen almost before Jo had finished and left quickly, yelling over his shoulder about being late for another appointment.

'No one says good-bye anymore,' Owen said. 'They go before you know they're gone.'

'Owen,' Jo started, 'why did you rope me into ten weeks when you know I need thirteen?'

'Timothy and I have history. That will be helpful when the time comes,' Owen explained. 'And the time will come, believe me.'

'What will happen?'

'Week ten, Timothy will play silly buggers. It's what makes him feel alive.'

'Oh no,' Jo moaned, 'I'm not good with silly buggers.'

'You don't have to be, you have me,' he replied with a smile before stretching back in his chair. 'I have to say, it's not like it used to be. Timothy's Dad, Fred, was an architect. We all used to hang out with one another. Me, Fred, other architects, other art dealers, collectors, artists. It was a gathering of the creative spirit.'

'Sounds wonderful,' Jo replied while feeling her body relaxing again, the tingling, the sagging.

'We would meet at each other's places on weekends, usually

drink a lot,' Owen chuckled. 'But now it's all five-minute deals over low-fat coffee. Where's the fun in that?'

'Fun?' Jo asked.

'Gallery contracts, insurance cover, sponsorship deals. The constant signing on dotted lines and then hurrying off somewhere else. We used to trust each other and support each other, and that was enough. Now it's complaining, networking and hurrying off,' the last word came out with spittle. He leaned down to look at the correspondence next to his chair from Kalimba's file clearing. 'A letter from Lila Carey dated 1976. Lila Carey,' he mused. 'What a sweetheart.'

'What an artist,' Jo added.

Lila Carey had been one of the few female painters recognised nationally in the 1950s and 60s. Her creative signature was the gentle strength captured of working-class women in inner-city Sydney.

'Technically superb,' Owen mused, 'but she also had that tender feeling just right. Talking of tender moments, nature calls.' Raising his body from the chair, Owen made his way to the bathroom just as Kalimba returned to the office.

'Do you know if Lila Carey is still painting?' Jo asked. 'I haven't seen anything of hers in years.'

'Don't know,' she replied, returning to her paper sorting. 'Given her age now, close to eighty, it's unlikely.'

Jo looked at the address on the letter Owen had picked up. 'Belvoir Street, Surrey Hills. That's just round the corner from me,' she laughed, 'Lila Carey and I could have been neighbours.'

'You still are, Owen says she hasn't moved in all this time. I'm sending some old photos back to her.'

Owen walked back into the room. 'Perhaps you wouldn't mind dropping the photographs off to Lila on your way home, Jo?'

'Really? Meet Lila Carey?' she said, her large eyes expanding further. 'Owen, it would be a privilege.'

'Excellent. I'll call to let her know you're coming. She'll be furious, of course. Doesn't like meeting new people these days, or old ones for that matter.'

'You'd better post the photos to her then,' Jo shrugged.

'Rubbish. I know artists need their isolation, but a good dealer can spot when to pull them out of it. Remember when you said you wanted twelve paintings for the show, and I said ten?'

'And you were right,' Jo nodded.

'Good, it's settled then,' Owen replied.

'Is Lila still painting?' she asked.

'Err, don't think so. The odd hobby daub maybe,' he said while looking around his desk. 'Kalimba, where are those snaps?'

***

The cottage and garden were like the children of freewheeling parents. Both had been loved but had become unruly. Jo had to fight through vines, spider webs and bowed agapanthus to get to the front steps, where she knocked loudly several times, as instructed. Just when her wrist began to throb, a clear, authoritative voice could be heard from the other side of the old walnut-stained door.

'Whoever is stupid enough to be still standing there, move on or I'll release the hounds. It's dinnertime.'

'It's three-thirty in the afternoon,' Jo replied, following Owen's instructions.

'Who are you to assume when it's dinnertime?'

'I have some photographs from Owen Marks. He called about half an hour ago to let you know I was coming. I'm Jo.'

'He did call, and I told him he could post the bloody things or haul his over-manicured bone bag down here himself.'

'Owen said you never let him inside.' He had also scripted this line for Jo.

As predicted, the door opened. 'Owen said what?' the woman asked, incredulous. 'The foolish man was only in here last Thursday.' Jo had to drop her vision to meet the eyes of Lila Carey. A grey bun with the fragility of a seeded dandelion head sat precariously on the back of the short woman's head. Accessorised head to toe by paint splatters, the purple t-shirt and black trousers were barely visible.

'Owen is getting forgetful,' Jo offered.

'Nonsense,' Lila snapped. 'He's just found a new excuse to get away with bad behaviour.' Lila squinted at Jo, 'You're an artist, aren't you?' she said.

'Well, yes, I…'

'In that case, you'd better come in,' Lila said with a sigh, disappearing down a hallway. Jo hurried after the speedy elderly.

'Where are the hounds?' she asked.

'They don't exist,' Lila answered back, 'but it's definitely dinnertime.' The smell of turpentine met them in the hallway. 'You like grappa?' the old woman asked.

Jo was led into an enormous studio. Completely unprepared, she released a gasp. Lila didn't seem to hear, too focused on moving even faster towards the antique chiffonier at the other end of the room. The path involved dodging the protruding corners of a number of enormous canvases sitting on easels. All were the same dimension, three metres high by one metre wide. More paintings were lined up on the floor along the walls. Each canvas was of a tall tree in dappled light, and each tree was of a different species: a eucalyptus, an oak, a flame tree, a silver birch, a pandanus. But when looked at closely, the tree was also a human figure. The mesmerising effect was almost holographic. Completely surrounded by the paintings, Jo saw herself in a forest, in a crowd, in a forest. There was enough work for at least one full-scale solo exhibition, with stockroom surplus. A collector would buy several, if not all, simply for the forest effect.

'I can't believe Owen's been telling tales about me,' Lila chattered as her bony hand grabbed the grappa bottle and two tumblers. 'He's one of the few I do allow in here. He should consider himself privileged.'

'He's seen all this?' Jo asked, still digesting the discovery.

'Of course.'

'When's the exhibition then?'

'There's no plan. And he knows not to blab about it. Now come and sit over here.' The old woman sat in one of two large leather armchairs. Both had paint smears of various colours over the arms and back. Large reference books–art, nature, religion, mythology, literature, architecture–were stacked around the chairs. With dexterous movement, the bottle top was off and the glasses half-filled with the transparent liquid. One glass was passed to Jo as she sank into the other chair.

'Cheers,' said Lila.

'Cheers,' she answered. Remembering the official purpose of the visit, Jo handed over the envelope. 'Here are your photographs.'

Lila took the envelope and threw it unopened onto a pile of sketches in the corner. After a moment of concentrated sipping, Lila said, 'I love dinnertime.' Jo winced at the grappa's pomace potency. *Italians. They overdo everything.*

Then Lila declared, 'They say I'm eccentric.'

'Do they?' Jo answered.

'The Oxford dictionary defines eccentric as…let me get this right,' Lila picked up the heavy tome nearby and flipped through the thin pages with gusto, 'here it is…not having its axis placed centrally, not circular.' She looked up at Jo, 'Not circular… We're all circular, aren't we? Molecularly speaking anyway.' She slammed the book closed in disgust. 'The subtext for "eccentric" is "crazy but manageable".' Jo braved another sip, watching Lila steadily over her glass. Lila frowned. 'Takes some chutzpah, following a crazy person into their home, unless you're crazy, of course.'

'Me? No…well, sometimes I don't know.'

'Good answer, for an artist,' the old woman nodded and smiled. 'Still, we can take comfort in the fact that while wondering if we have lost our minds, we are utilising some rational faculty. So, who had dementia?' Lila asked abruptly.

'Sorry?'

'Someone close to you, someone in the family, had dementia.'

'How did you know?'

'Takes one to know one,' Lila said.

'Well,' Jo started, 'my grandmother when I was ten.' Lila nodded but said nothing. 'Then three years ago my mother died after…with…Alzheimer's.'

'Watching someone you love disappear while they have the nerve to still look like they're there. It's tough. My Gordon was like that. I was furious with him, but he couldn't help it.'

'What happened?'

'He died,' Lila said with a flick of the hand.

'I'm sorry.'

'Don't be. It was a godsend for the man. Me too, I suppose,' she shrugged. 'We all die sometime, right? Death is…reliable.'

'Like taxes.' Jo tilted her glass to the light coming through the window.

'There are some people who never pay taxes.'

'Struggling artists?' Jo asked.

'No, usually wealthy art collectors,' she replied. 'Interestingly, their wives have paid taxes. Wives who haven't worked a day in their lives.'

'They call that creative accountancy, don't they?'

'There's nothing creative about it,' Lila shook her head as she placed her empty tumbler down on the floor. 'They are merely skilled jugglers.'

Jo looked around at the paintings. 'Compared to you, Lila,' she said, 'I'm wondering whether I should have become an accountant.'

'Know one thing, Jo,' Lila said, pointing her rough, bony finger at her. 'You are an artist. Hold onto that fact as if it were the only rope to sanity, regardless of how many people tell you that the rope doesn't exist. And believe me, they will come.'

***

'Then what did the old bat say?'

'Don't call her that,' Jo reproached. 'Lila's incredible.'

Nora then smiled broadly to apply cherry rouge on her lips. 'I'm being facetious.'

'You don't have to listen if you don't want to.'

'But I do, I do,' Nora glanced at her watch. 'At least until Heath arrives. He's already half an hour late. Ten more minutes and he's dead meat.'

'Lila's a lot like you, actually.'

'Tell me more about this incredible person.'

Jo drew her knees up under her chin. 'The paintings I saw in that studio were astonishing.'

'Do you tell other people how amazing I am?'

'Her work now is even better than what she's famous for,' Jo persisted.

'Often the way isn't it? There are Vincent Van Goghs everywhere with ears missing, blood everywhere and studios full of incredible….' Nora stopped. She recognised her own speech. Earlier, it had been said about Jo, during the Unfashionable Period. They both remember it.

'No one knows about these paintings,' Jo intercepted, 'except for Owen.'

'Can't be much of a gallery dealer if he's got a goldmine at his feet and he's doing nothing about it.'

'Lila's asked him to hold off.' Jo explained, touched by Owen's integrity. Indeed, the gallery director had a goldmine within reach, but the artist's wishes came first. Usually. *Ten weeks*, Jo thought.

Nora's phone rang. 'That'll be Mr Dead Meat.' She tapped and yelled, 'You're late, you bastard.'

Then Jo's phone rang. It was Kalimba 'Owen's in hospital, Jo. It's serious.'

'You're dead meat!' Nora yelled.

***

Owen was still unconscious when they arrived. A friend had found him alone in his apartment two days before. According to the scans, there had been a large benign tumour in his brain, causing complications. 'The surgery went reasonably well,' the nurse explained. 'There is hope for Owen regaining full consciousness. When that may happen, however, we don't know.'

Nora decided to visit with Jo, as the idea of talking at a man rather than with one held a greater attraction. Owen had a strange, smug expression fixed on his face.

'At least he doesn't look like he's in pain,' Jo said.

'Pain? He looks like he's fresh from a good time at Club Wet, is what he does.' Nora chuckled. 'Don't think we don't know what you get up to, naughty Owen.' Jo cringed, regretting sharing that piece of gossip.

After talking to Owen about Lila's paintings, reading some Rumi poetry from Jo's phone, and the latest celebrity gossip from Nora's, in between taking shuttle runs for vending machine coffee and junk snacks, they decided it was time to go. Jo leant over to whisper, 'If you're not out of this coma by week ten when Timothy Banks plays silly buggers, I'll finish you off myself.' Gently squeezing his arm, she said, 'Sleep tight,' and walked out the door, absently rubbing her hand.

'For the love of god, Jo,' Nora said. 'Would you just see a doctor about it?'

Jo was shocked. 'My wrist?'

'Yes, your bloody wrist. What else?'

My mind? She wondered. Jo hadn't even thought about a doctor for her wrist. Suffering in poverty had been her jam for so long the idea of paying for medical assistance was up there with a Caribbean cruise. Up there and out of reach. 'Okay,' she said, staring at her cradled appendage like it was a neglected pet. 'I will.'

***

Timothy Banks accepted Jo's commission concept at first submission. She had worked quickly on it to buy herself an extra week of painting time, but she wasn't surprised that he had accepted it. The painting was of an architect. A computer was positioned on the left-hand side of the composition, dominating the drawing board in the background with blueprints tacked on the walls, corners curling in the half-light. Takeaway wrappers were scattered across the floor.

'The evolution from manual draftsmanship to the wonders of CAD,' Timothy gushed. 'The designer hard at work, who doesn't even have time to eat properly.'

Jo saw the abandoned drawing board as a death of something honourable and the takeaway wrappers as a symbol of manmade rubbish covering the surface of the natural environment, but she didn't include that in the concept brief. Instead, she had him sign the approval and locked herself into the studio, wrist in a splint from the doctor for the onslaught. Of course, she nodded when the doctor said, "Take this calcium, have lots of rest and keep your wrist above heart level." The deadline only allowed interruptions for sleeping, eating, taking calcium supplements and anti-inflammatories, and visiting Owen, who maintained the same smug expression.

During the second visit, Jo told Owen that she had returned to Lila's house to inform her about his health. Unfortunately, no amount of knocking had summoned the woman, so a short letter was slipped under the door explaining the situation, her phone number added to the bottom. No call came, and there was no sign Lila had visited Owen's bedside.

Ten weeks from the day of concept approval, however, Timothy Banks called Jo's number.

'I have a piece of paper here that says you have a finished painting for me.'

'It's almost done, just a few more days. I got the concept to you a week early, remember?'

'I have a contract that you signed,' he replied. 'We need to install tomorrow. I've called the gallery. They know all about it.'

'So you know Owen's fine.'

'Fine?' he said. 'No, I heard he was in hospital.'

'He's in a coma. But Owen's fine because he's not listening to this.'

'At least he's not in pain,' Timothy said, 'unlike me.'

Jo rubbed her throbbing wrist. 'I can't finish it in one day just because you -'

'There is the alternative.'

'And what might that be?'

'As per the contract, you pay the expenses of the delay: the cancellation of the launch, the re-launch, etcetera. It's an ad campaign worth thousands of dollars.'

'But I don't have thousands of dollars.'

'After a sell-out show like yours?' he snorted. 'I saw the prices.'

'I don't have the money.'

'It's your call,' Timothy replied. 'I'll email you the expenses sheet within in the next half hour. It will give you an opportunity to assess your options. Let's meet tomorrow afternoon at three at Edifice. You either have in your hand a painting or a cheque.'

For five minutes, Jo stared into space, much like the subjects in her paintings. Then the phone rumbled its vibration in her hand, the screen flashing an unfamiliar number.

'Hello?'

'If your reception drops out for even a second, I'm hanging up,' the voice warned. 'I hate mobile phones.'

The voice was unmistakable. 'Lila, you got my letter about Owen?'

'Yes, but I'm calling about a letter *from* Owen. It was more of a self-important piece of twaddle, actually.'

'He's out of the coma?' Her heart lifted at the miracle timing.

'No, he's still there. This note was in the envelope you gave me along with the photographs,' Lila continued. 'I opened it a couple of weeks back. Owen was bragging about just snaffling a commission between you and Timothy Banks. When I heard Owen was in hospital, I told the gallery to call me when little Timmy starts playing...what did Owen always call it?'

'Silly buggers?'

'That's it,' Lila said. 'Owen's assistant...what's her name?'

'Kalimba.'

'Yes, Kalimba. Nice girl. Well, she just called me, saying that Timothy was after your mobile number. I figure he's just threatened all manner of ridiculous things.'

'Yes, that's pretty accurate.'

'How much time do you need to deliver the painting?'

'Just another week. I'm almost there.'

'When's the meeting with Timothy?'

'Tomorrow afternoon at three,' Jo replied. 'It's at Edifice in the city.'

'Organise a taxi pick me up on the way,' she said. 'Or one of those Doobers.'

'An Uber?'

'Just kidding,' she chuckled. 'I know what Uber is. I take them all the time'

'That's really sweet, Lila, but I was thinking I might need a lawyer.'

'Two things you need to know,' Lila said. 'One is that there's nothing sweet about me. And two, you won't need a lawyer.'

'I won't?'

'What did you say? Did you just drop out?' Lila yelled.

'Why won't I need a lawyer, Lila?' Jo said loudly.

'Can't hear anything. I'm hanging up. See you tomorrow.'

No one says goodbye anymore, Jo thought. They go before you know they're gone.

***

'Lila Carey? What a delightful surprise,' Timothy Banks exclaimed. 'I thought you were dead.'

'And I thought you were intelligent.'

'Ah,' he faltered, holding out his hand to shake Lila's.

She didn't accept it.

They were standing in the finished foyer, surrounded by grey granite, glass, and stainless steel. And three minimalist black leather sofas the shape of kidney beans. All that was missing was a focal work of art. A drill could be heard from above, somewhere in the ceiling.

'Would you like to sit down?' Timothy gestured to the nearest couch. 'Have a latte, perhaps?'

Lila ignored both offers. 'It's time to grow up, Timmy.'

'I beg your pardon?'

Jo stood by silently and began scrolling for *Top cheapest lawyers Sydney*.

'Your father is dead,' Lila said, 'but he's turning in his grave as we speak.'

'I know you and Dad were close, but I am my own person, Lila.'

'Fred commissioned fourteen paintings from me, Timothy, and hundreds more from other emerging artists. He was integral in creating and sustaining the art lifeblood of this city.' Jo had one eye on the Greek play before her and one on Google search.

'I have fond memories of him, too,' he said. 'But these are different times.' The condescension was so thick it could have been used as an industrial surface product.

'The difference is that when architects like you organise a commission, it's an afterthought. You leave it to the last minute and torture creativity with insane deadlines, threaten artists with bankruptcy before they're even out of the red.'

'Instead of making wild judgements, Lila, let's focus on the facts.' Timothy looked at Jo for the first time that day. But Lila kept talking.

'Here are the facts,' she said. 'Owen Marks is part of the contractual agreement. He's currently unconscious so, legally, the contract period is suspended due to negotiations being unable to proceed as per the stipulations in the contract regarding delivery of the painting. That's Owen's job.' Jo stopped scrolling. Lila continued. 'Jo will be ready to deliver in two weeks, possibly one if you behave like a gentleman. So you better not play…what is it?'

'Silly buggers,' Jo whispered.

'…silly buggers in that time.'

'Or what, Lila?' Timothy sneered.

'I'll tell your mother.'

Timothy laughed, 'You'll tell my mother I'm forcing an artist to deliver as per a contractual agreement.'

'No, I'll tell her about what you did to your little brother when you were twelve.'

The Greek play just got bigger. And Timothy's pride turned into something much smaller. 'Dad told you about that?'

'In those days, business relationships were different. We drank together, laughed together, told each other everything,' she said. 'So you're right, Timothy, these are different times. But I'm still alive.'

*   *   *

'Lila, that was incredible,' Jo said, trying to keep up with the woman who was striding out of the building. 'Thank you so much.'

'It was a pleasure to put that little runt back in his place.'

'What on earth did he do to his brother?' Jo asked as they caught a taxi idling nearby. Lila didn't answer but instead scrambled into the back seat. At that moment, Jo's mobile phone rang. It was the gallery with news that Owen had just regained consciousness. He was doing well, regaining all faculties, but wouldn't accept visitors until the following day. He needed his sleep, the doctor had said.

'Sleep?' Lila scoffed, 'what on earth do they think he's been doing for the last ten weeks?'

When the taxi pulled up outside Lila's house, she announced it was dinnertime. 'Coming in?' Lila threw some dollar notes at the driver and made her way towards the door.

Jo looked at her watch. It was three-thirty. Even though the studio beckoned, a small celebration seemed in order. When she followed Lila into the studio, however, Jo almost screamed. Every canvas had been freshly whitewashed, every work of art gone.

'Your beautiful paintings, what happened?' she spun around, disbelieving.

'They're just hiding,' Lila replied. 'Don't worry, dear, I'll paint others over the top. Good Belgian linen is expensive, you know.'

'But those paintings were incredible,' she stammered. 'I know Owen would have bought you more linen.'

'Owen?' Lila laughed, appearing as demented as she had in the beginning. 'Well, yes, he probably would, wouldn't he?' Lila shook her head firmly, her bun holding on precariously. 'No, if he bought the linen, I would have to exhibit them.' Jo looked at her, disbelieving. Lila sat down with both glasses and nodded to the other chair. Jo walked tentatively past the white canvases as if they were ghosts. Lila handed over the tumbler before sinking into the leather.

'The world's had enough of me, and I of it,' she said. 'Now don't look so miserable. It's emancipating.'

'I don't get it,' Jo said, wincing at her glass again after feeling the grappa burn her throat.

'It's all very simple, my dear,' Lila winked while taking a sip. 'These aren't for anyone else.'

'Not for anyone else at all?' Jo took another sip and caught the burn again, causing a cough.

'For no one else,' Lila repeated, then took a hefty swig and smiled. The woman clearly had practice. Every day at three-thirty.

'But don't you want to share them?' Jo asked, incredulous. 'That was a whole exhibition.'

She shook her head, then leaned forward. 'This is what you have to understand, Jo.' Jo leant in towards her, listening deeply. Lila continued. 'This, you see, this…'

'Yes?' Jo urged.

'This is my time.'

CONFESSIONS OF THE BODY

[Drop Cookie]

Most people recall when sack-em-up Santa was exposed as a sham. Some even remember the Easter Bunny, a once liberal chocolate distributor, becoming merely a mascot for Jesus' existential dosey-doh. I will always remember when the pet canary died. As the rigor mortis set in, my parents came clean.

'We all die,' my father mumbled while wrapping up the bird in newspaper like battered barramundi.

'Usually later...rather than sooner,' my mother added helpfully. Truth tends to be cold, and on that summer's day it could have snowed. Bertie was dead. But more importantly, one day we were all going to be wrapped in newspaper and buried next to the rhododendron behind the compost.

You wouldn't think it could get much worse than that. However, there was one thing they left out. One thing you quietly learn on your own while ducking and weaving from the all-hands reaper and that ominous rhododendron. I only grasped it recently and wonder why no one mentioned it before.

It's widely assumed if you get sick the next thing to do is get cured. Problem, solution. When I became ill as a child, I went to bed, drank lots of fluids, and popped the pills when necessary. Once my illness was beyond my mother's medicinal boundaries. The smiling doctor appeared at my bedroom door wielding a prescribed chemical mallet. After a couple of days, I was back to normal.

My mother was the clinic manager for a local doctor. She probably used her wiles to lure her boss into this house visit, figuring 'home turf' gave her an advantage. Being a clinic manager gave her the impression she was qualified to diagnose and treat our family. Smuggling home free pharmaceutical samples from sales-hungry drug company reps, she tended to our medicine cabinet as if it was a shrine. If nothing else, her success average was solid, but I developed a natural degree of fear whenever I heard the light rattle of pills or the gentle pop from a blister pack.

As patients, my parents represented both ends of the temperament scale. My mother was never sick while I was a child. Either that or she out-faked Santa and Easter Bunny by a wholesome mile. Since my promotion to adulthood, she moved onto demonstrating gentle sniffing and feeling her own forehead when precariously near the deathbed. My father, on the other hand, was an unbearable hypochondriac whose pitiful plays for attention became the family joke. Well, until he got cancer. Thankfully he recovered, allowing Mum and I to look upon what happened as a slap on the wrist from God for him complaining so much. My father must have caught a whiff of it, too. One Sunday afternoon, when Mum had gone out, Dad accidentally attacked his own shins with the garden whipper-snipper. How he managed to do so much damage was uncertain. I watched in horror as his macerated limbs bled like a sub-tropical cascade while he sipped his beer on the veranda. I didn't know what was worse, the graphic blood loss or the peculiar smile on his face, reminding me of Norman Bates.

As a child, I was entitled to one check-up every third year with our mother's boss. It was all to do with appearances. She figured it would look suspicious if her child never saw a doctor. A professionally certified one, that was. During these times she sat next to whoever was being inspected, while the other child played in the waiting room with saliva-soaked, bacteria-riddled toys. My mother's hands clenched together, waiting for the doctor to discover something she missed. It was torturous for all of us. There were lots of 'mmm's and 'interesting's as he peered and prodded. But no matter how ponderable I was, he never did find anything medically amiss. When we returned home after the appointment, regardless of the time of day, my mother would kick off her heels and smugly treat herself to an obscenely large whiskey.

Moving away from home, a small city of half a million, to a bigger city with more study and job opportunities was not shocking to my parents, or even our broader community. Leaving the nest was expected. Not just to the next tree but to a whole other forest. It was probably my most proactive act to date. Independence to live life on my own terms. Doing what exactly, I wasn't sure.

My old school friends had clear goals with defined paths to get there. I watched them follow their respective yellow brick roads, backpacks already filled with intelligence, compassion, and courage, heading off toward horizons imperceptible to me. My asphalt path was short. I took an office administration job at the Water Authority, which was essentially doggy paddling until an epiphany decided to visit. In the meantime, I made new friends who were more floating office worker types like me.

We hung out in cafes and bars. For health, I jogged around the neighbourhood a couple of times a week, played beach cricket or park frisbee on weekends with my ambition-free tribe. Later, we would go out to hear live music or to the movies. Gandhi once said, 'Live simply so that others simply live.' That was my excuse and I stuck firmly to it. I did read books. Maybe not high-end literature, but mysteries, romances, even some chick lit with 'a message'. When feeling creative, I designed god-awful cocktails at home for whoever was game to be my guinea pig. Was I wasting my life away? Maybe. Was I regretting it? Not one bit. As 'lite' as my life was, it was busy enough, interesting enough, and fun enough. Until it wasn't.

I met Gus at a picnic. The weather turned mid-afternoon, but it was just enough time to get to know him. The basics, at least. Gus worked at his dad's trophy business, which could be his one day. That is, if the mega-national awards and trophies companies don't chew them up and spit them out. And if Gus wanted the business.

'There's no pressure,' Gus said. 'Only if I want it. Dad's great like that.'

'Do you want it?'

'Dunno,' Gus said, shrugging. 'Don't have to make any big decisions now.'

It was love at first shrug. He was kind, non-judgemental and made me laugh. We hung out well together, and he fitted right in with my tribe. Easy. Effortless.

Some things in life are not effortless. I recall being allergic to seafood around the age of six. Or did I just tell everyone that because it tasted like a mixture of steel and deteriorating spinach? Seafood you can avoid - like the plague - and mosey on. But nothing specific in my upbringing prepared me for 'Limbo Health Management'. As an expert on non-exertion, it came as a surprise when fatigue landed on me like an invisible piano. Like so many others in my orbit that winter, I got a virus. Home tests proved it wasn't COVID. It was something else. But when the worst was over (or so I thought), I was left in a post-viral haze, much like long COVID. News reports suggested fatigue for a few days after a virus, any virus, was common these days. I wasn't concerned. Some time on the couch suited me fine. I kept forgetting where I put my phone, which drove me bat crazy until I didn't care anymore. Gus came around regularly after work to help with cooking, cleaning, and finding my phone. He was an angel dressed in jeans and surf t-shirts. After my phone was found and domestic basics were done, I intercepted his industry with a kiss and sent him away to participate in the outside world. Talking was exhausting. Even watching a movie with another person took it out of me. I gave strict instructions for friends not to visit, explaining I fully intended to emerge as a human butterfly soon enough.

'I need stories,' I explained to Gus. 'You are not my war correspondent, but my entertainment correspondent. Bring back reports,' I commanded with a grin. Which he did. I heard how our buddy Alex received a promotion he didn't want because his manager got fired for taking too much initiative. And our friend Kim, a casual employee at a jeans shop, had a date with a lawyer who worked in social justice. The guy had a side-hustle in protesting clothing manufacturing in Asia. Kim tried to move the conversation onto community gardens, but her date wouldn't have it. The evening got ugly. Then extremely passionate.

Watching Gus giving his reports, I wondered how I could feel so crap and so lucky at the same time. The emotion ran through me, and I burst into tears. Somehow, for all the fatigue, my body still found the energy for crying. A lot. I had somehow inherited the emotional stability of a Big Brother contestant. It was embarrassing. I wasn't feeling sad. I wasn't feeling anything apart from perhaps a little frustrated looking for my phone. I tried to get the crying done on my own throughout the day, so I was Sahara-safe by the time Gus came around. But it didn't always work. Fortunately, Gus was one of those guys who was relaxed around crying women. And he believed me when I said, 'I'm fine. Tired, but fine.' We even laughed about it.

As Gus served up the chicken soup he'd just made, I asked, 'What kind of soup do chickens have when they feel under the weather?'

'Hey, I made this soup for you to feel better. Not for me to feel worse.'

'Sorry,' I said, trying not to cry while trying to find something to say that might redeem me. 'I have a better question. Two, actually.'

'I'm game,' he said, blowing on his spoon.

'Do award-makers have an award ceremony for the best award-making business? And if so, what do the awards look like?'

'The answers are: 'no' and 'incredible',' he said. I chuckled into my soup, glad we were back on track. 'I have a question for you, madam,' he said, looking square at me.

'Yes?' I asked, feeling the room's levity sink.

'When are you going to the doctor?'

'Soon, promise.'

'Not soon. Call tomorrow.'

'And what if I don't?' I contested.

'Or I'll tell your mother what's going on with you.' I looked at the man with new found respect. He was nice, but no pushover.

I made the appointment, spent the day feeling exhausted just from that one task. Gus came over and we ate dinner together as always. I reported my good behaviour and he just nodded, no fuss. The next day Gus left for work before I was awake. But I found on the coffee table a sort of upcycled miniature sculpture. A box of penne sitting on a box of cotton buds with my nail polish bottle (blossom pink) on the very top. Leaning on the penne was a small white card, upon which perfectly scribed text was written my name, then underneath: 'Award for Making Doctor's Appointment'. I couldn't help but smile. It was my first ever trophy.

Gus insisted he was coming with me to the medical clinic, but I delivered an emphatic 'No'. Those netball trophies were not going to etch themselves, I said. And I wasn't completely useless. Was I?

'Who took the 'practical' out of medical practitioner?' I hear people cry, usually those who call the office 'home'. While in the waiting room of the doctor's surgery (hundreds of kilometres away from my mother's), I witnessed a corporate executive have a hernia when the GP recommended three days' rest. The beige walls must have been made of rice cakes because anyone in the waiting room could hear everything. I made a mental note to whisper when my number came up, even if it meant pretending to have a cold.

'I can't have a break now,' the patient whined like a child fighting off bedtime. I understood his panic. If the *deal* could be put to bed it would mean an early cashed-up retirement. He could be as sick as he likes then. I understood it but didn't have the same concerns. I had no big business cooking. I just wanted to be healthy again so I could drink copious amounts of booze, devour chocolate by the box full, and stay up late throwing my skeletal structure out on the dance floor. Also, to enjoy my 'special time' with Gus. That was energy well worth spending.

'I caught the same virus everyone in the office had,' I whispered to Dr McIntyre. Dr McIntyre was a woman in a pressed blue shirt and slacks (yes, slacks) who couldn't look amusing if dressed in a bunny onesie. 'But my co-workers were fine after a day or two. Me? I can't shake the bugger.'

'What's wrong with your voice?' Dr McIntyre asked.

'Nothing. I just like privacy.' My eyes shifted to the wall dividing us from the waiting room. 'Seriously, they can hear everything.'

'They can?' the doctor looked at me sideways, clearly wondering if I required a psych consult. I insisted on a demonstration. I kept talking about nothing, 'Nothing in particular, I'm talking, nothing, nothing, nothing," I said over and over as McIntyre sat in the waiting room until she returned.

'But in here,' she said, 'I can't hear anyone in the waiting room.'

'Weird, right?' I whispered.

'Yes,' she agreed. 'Now…back to your fatigue,' she whispered back. 'ME/CFS is common among Type As.'

'ME/CFS?'

'Myalgic encephalomyelitis forward-slash chronic fatigue syndrome'

'Chronic fatigue?' I repeated, unable to repeat the rest. It sounded like a blowfly trapped in a toilet. I remember once joking over a frozen mojito I was made for chronic fatigue. Doing bugger-all was my area of expertise. McIntyre waited patiently as my shame sank in. Then I asked. 'What is a Type A?'

'High achiever personality trait.'

I burst out laughing and then began to cry for no reason. 'That's not me,' I mumbled through my tears.

'Let's not rush into theories,' she said pushing a tissue box in my direction, then sitting back in her chair as if trying to avoid a crying contagion. 'We need to run some tests.' To be honest, I quite enjoy medical tests. No study involved. I don't have to do anything special to score a result except show up. Plus, the result isn't really my fault.

At my second appointment, McIntyre shuffled the pathology reports like a pack of cards and gave a deep sigh. Mysteries to McIntyre has the same effect as kryptonite to Superman. And I was one big chunk of mystery beaming away opposite her. She grimaced in return, then pushed headlong into prescribing antibiotics the size of mini footballs.

'Let's see how they go over the next few weeks,' she said, guiding me out the door. Weeks passed. Nothing changed, except I got a cold.

I had returned to work because I needed money for eating, rent and online clairvoyant sessions (while providing no helpful answers, the loving focus on my wellbeing was proving addictive). But looking awake at work, operating with a functioning memory and enough mojo to muster any level of productivity was a struggle, even for someone deeply camouflaged in administrative mid-grey like me. Thankfully, news (both official and gossip) discussing the reality of long-COVID, and the puzzle of new viruses kept my boss at bay. I came home, collapsed in front of Gus, who was laughing less and frowning more.

'You can't keep going like this,' he said.

'You can't keep going like this,' I replied.

'What do you mean?'

'Leave and don't come back. Please,' I said rubbing my eyes, trying to hold the tears back. 'I'm as boring as a…I dunno.' I was too tired to conjure a metaphor. 'Seriously, Gus. The guilt is crushing me.'

'What and not find out how it ends? You're crazy,' he smiled, rubbing my back. 'Okay, so I was thinking it's time for a lateral approach. Let's try natural medicine.' I stared at him for a while, in awe of how he brushed my guilt play to the side so fast. Impressive.

'Have you ever tried natural medicine?' I asked.

'No,' he said. 'But that doesn't mean it's not worthwhile, right?' I had no energy to argue. Gus googled, made appointments, and drove me to clinics with waiting rooms that looked more like harems. Naturopaths, acupuncturists, herbalists, and health centres with big green logos that would give a frog like Kermit some heart. It took a bit longer for me. No one was sure what was wrong, except for my liver-chi stagnation. But I was informed most people in the Western world suffer from liver-chi stagnation. So, no prizes there. I swallowed disgusting herbal concoctions in a similar fashion to the miniature footballs.

Members of my tribe began to drift in and out of my apartment. No more than two at a time. They didn't stay long, but I got hugs and momentary tv sit-com companions. They usually left some supermarket-purchased pre-cooked meals in the fridge. My people weren't the casserole-cooking kind. And the supermarket meals were surprisingly delicious. The flow of visitations was like a gentle ballet, no doubt choreographed by Gus.

One morning I woke to another assembly on my coffee table. This time it was my shampoo bottle, sitting on a box of sea salt flakes, with a full bulb of garlic on the top. Again, there was a card. And again, my name had been written in perfect script, but this time underneath was: 'Award for Drinking Poxy Herb Stuff'.

There was some change from the poxy herbal stuff. Depending on the day, I could find my phone myself. But more fundamental strategies still had to be put into action. I had been told by my acupuncturist that our health begins in the gut and was recommended to visit a highly regarded nutritionist. Having no fight left in me, I dutifully did was I was told. My diet radically changed. Everything I enjoyed was shafted, left with the sort of meals you would get in the womb. This wasn't just for a few weeks, or a couple of months. We're talking years. Maybe FOREVER. Avoid all added sugars, by-pass all carbohydrates. It was the 'No alcohol' statement that sent me foetal. Life is certainly a cycle. The nutritionist noticed my reaction, mentioned 'stress level monitoring,' and packed me off to a psychologist.

The psychologist had plush carpet and nice, comfy chairs. Noticing the toys in the corner, I asked how parents could concentrate on a session with their children playing in the room. Apparently, the toys were for the adults. I had great fun for the whole hour, until I got the bill. I had heard that childcare was expensive. It looked like my inner child was going to have abandonment issues for a long time to come.

I was still wondering how long Gus was going to stick around for a girlfriend who belongs in a black and white Eastern European indie film where nothing happens.

'Bok,' I said as he walked through my front door in one afternoon. By now he had a key as I wasn't always awake when he came. He didn't seem to mind.

'Bok?'

'That's "hi" in Croatian,' I said, pointing to Google Translate on my phone.

'Bok backatcha,' he said, giving me a kiss then joining me on the couch. 'Guess what? I've found a hybrid.'

'I've always wanted to find a hybrid,' I said. 'Actually… I've always wanted to be a hybrid. Maybe your hybrid could teach me?'

'You want to be a GP who is also a qualified herbalist?'

'Not that kind of hybrid. Sounds like too much work.'

'Agreed,' Gus replied. 'But visiting one could mean our luck has doubled.'

When men say, 'We're pregnant', women generally wish to take to the gent with a baseball bat. But when you are chronically ill, and your fella speaks in terms of 'we' and 'our' you want to chain them him to the furniture so they never leave you. Or, at least, that's how I felt.

'But getting into these Integrated Medical Practitioners, can be tricky,' he said. 'I've been told they're in high demand.' Who was Gus talking with to get this information? Probably everyone who crossed his path. A weird combination of extreme embarrassment and gratitude filled me. So, of course, I began crying. Gus rubbed my shoulders with one hand while searching for the online booking page with the other. We found one appointment space free and nabbed it. After high-fiving, Gus was still ecstatic. I crawled into bed. The next morning my beloved had left another creation. My yet-to-be-burned fat candle was sitting on a square tissue box, with my antique inkwell on the very top. The card, with my name, said: 'Award for Doing Very Little – For Your Health'.

The hybrid GP cleaned the slate and started again. Which meant another series of tests, leading to another doctorial shrug. The kind of shrug that was becoming increasingly anxiety-provoking.

'I'll pay good money for a placebo that works,' I pleaded.

The hybrid was too busy frowning at my file. 'Whatever it is, you're going have to give up work indefinitely,' he said, dragging his eyes away from the screen to look at the cause of his problem. Me.

'But without a diagnosis I can't receive the government support I need to give up work,' I explained. 'And that really messes with my nutritionist's diet plan.'

'How so?'

'I can't afford to eat.'

The gods heeded the call of my hybrid. The next day, my boss drew the line. Tiring of my desk absences, either because I was at one of my endless medical appointments or curled up under the desk, the terms of my employment contract were not being met. Being an insecure fellow with his own set of inner-child abandonment issues, I was fired.

Everyone in my tribe who heard the news proclaimed I should contest for unfair dismissal. It was easy to suggest, particularly in a righteous manner, but very hard to action. Being champions of the laissez-fare, I knew they would never do it - and they had their health. How could I contest the Water Authority with a brain like cold mashed potato and the body of an inert slinky?

With all the extra medical expenses, my savings had been reduced to two digits (index and middle finger). Salutes withstanding, I fast became the inverse to Baden Powell. Up the river without a paddle, unwell and unemployed. All I really wanted was a drink and a chockie.

Life's crises sometimes lead us to doing things that we never thought we would do, like asking my mother for medical advice. It was the necessary precursor to asking for money. She lived two states away, so our lengthy consults were over the phone. Remarkably, after much research and the posting of tablets past their use-by dates, even my mother had to admit I was a medical enigma. When my dad transferred some emergency funds into my bank account, I knew that she was pouring her entire supply of whiskey down the sink.

My tribe brought supermarket soup. The other pre-cooked meals had something in them I wasn't supposed to be eating. Again, this shift was Gus at work for my greater good. What surprised us both was the cheque presented by one member, on behalf of the group. They had combined their coin for a generous sum to help me through whatever this was. My tears. Oh god, my tears. Then Gus offered what I could not possibly request. For him to 'officially' move in.

'I'm pretty much living here anyway. Your rent is the same as mine is… almost.'

'I'll pay you back.'

'There's nothing to pay back. I want to be with you.'

Through yet another dam-busting surge of tears, I had to ask, 'Why (sob) on earth (sob) for?'

'You are my home. Even when you were well, you were my home. And, through this crap time, I realised something about what I want to do.'

'Don't tell me,' I held up my hand. 'Upcycling sculptor.'

'No,' he said giving me a gentle shove.

'Why?' I said, my face solemn. 'You're really creative with my trophies.'

'Thanks, but no. I realised I want to work in Aged Care,' he said with a triumphant smile. It was not my finest moment. But much like my tears, my laughter was uncontrollable. I pushed my face into the couch pillow to try to stop, or at least mute myself. 'You find it FUNNY?' Gus yelled at me, horrified at what was happening.

I took some deep breaths and had some false starts before I could explain myself. 'You've got to see it from my per-(breath)-spective. What you said (breath) is not exactly a compliment.'

'What do you mean?'

Gus was not always the sharpest tool, but the man had a heart that overrode hardware supplies. 'Do you not see? (breath) I am an aged person in all but age.' I couldn't hold it in anymore. There was another bout of laughter, then I added, 'Why couldn't you have said 'troubled youth'?' I went to lie down on the couch, howl some more before I was able to take more breaths to tone myself down.

'You are not like an old person,' Gus said, wounded. 'That's not what I meant.'

I wiped my tears with my dressing gown sleeve and said, 'I know,' while patting him on the knee, just like an old person which made him laugh.

'Seriously, you are nothing like an old person,' he said with a grin appearing on his face. 'You have no idea what it's taken for me to hold myself back from you through all this. Your legs slipping in and out of view from that dressing gown. It's not been easy.'

'Seriously?' I said, looking at my legs with new appreciation.

'Seriously,' he said patting my knee, but not like an old person. The move inspired a session on the couch that took us both by surprise. Not long, but long enough.

'Back to seriously,' I said, pulling my robe back on and touching his face. 'You are born to be in caring. You are a natural.'

'You see it?'

'Of course, I do.'

'The pay will probably be crap,' he frowned while staring at the coffee table.

'But caring is more important than caring about that,' I said. Then a strange thing happened. I felt a little surge of something. Not laughter. Not tears. Ambition. Gus saw something shift in me and had to ask, 'What is it?'

'This is going to sound stupid...'

'You're in good company,' he smiled.

'But I just caught a glimpse of what I want to do.'

'Don't tell me.' He held up his hand. 'Take over my dad's business?'

'No, sorry.'

'That's okay. It's slowly tanking anyway.'

'Is it?'

'He will be relieved I'm getting out of it. There's just enough work for one of us now.'

'I didn't know.'

'I didn't tell you.'

'It's okay to tell me these things,' I said, then faltered. 'No, it's more than okay. It's really important. Otherwise, you're in my life but I'm not in yours. Tell me things.'

'Okay, I will,' Gus nodded, recognising my point. 'So, what is it you want to do?'

'I want to get a better paying job. In admin still, but better. More responsibility.' I held up my hand before he interjected. 'Yes, Gus. When I'm better.'

My first epiphany was that one day we are all going to be wrapped in newspaper and buried next to the rhododendron behind the compost. My second was that life is about caring, whether you're in aged care, administration or simply needing to spend your days on the couch. You may never get the result you want from caring for others, let alone a trophy for it, but it is the fertiliser for our health. The fuel for our happiness. And guess what? It doesn't take much. It's easy. It can even be, dare I say it, effortless.

TAXI OUTLAW

[Chocolate Crackle Cookies]

I'd put money on it. At least eighty percent of people think they are a bit different from the rest. They see the world and play their part in it. But, on the sly, something else is going on. They might think they're missing something, or they think they are better. Or they haven't made up their mind whether they are better or worse, or they don't care. They just feel a step away from what's going on around them. Truth is, we're all blood-and-bone snowflakes. We are all different. But people at work often notice a difference in me.

'You're a bit different, aren't you?' my current passenger says. He's fresh from a sailing club lunch. It's a nice day, early spring. Wearing a navy-blue reefer jacket, the tubby man is red faced more from decades of therapeutic beers than pulling ropes on deck. He's smiling while – I suspect – batting away the thought of impending retirement. The status and purpose of work slipping away from his fat, red grip. I shouldn't assume, I correct myself.

'What's it like driving a taxi these days, with Uber and all?' he says.

'Good,' I say. 'Always busy enough.'

'Being a woman, you have to be careful,' he says, while supressing a burp. 'Don't suppose you take the night shifts.'

'Sometimes I do,' I say with a smile.

'Yeah?' he looks at me, almost offended. How did I have to gall to think I was safe from his gender?

These questions and comments are common. Unsurprising. Predictable.

But being a woman who drives a taxi in Sydney doesn't make me all that different. There are more of us than you might think. I'm also an artist. A female taxi-driving artist. Does that make me different? I also break the law on a daily, or nightly, basis. How many people do that?

I drive a bog-standard silver Toyota Camry. It's a Goldilocks car. Big enough, small enough. The silver colour hides the dirt better than any other colour. I focus on keeping the black interior clean and odour-free. I can't stand those chemical air fresheners. Instead, I always keep a cloth bag of charcoal pellets under the front car seats. If someone has serious body odour or brings fried food in, my go-to is burning natural incense before picking up the next passenger. Then, after I've finished my shift, I sit a bowl of vinegar in the backseat until I start again.

For ambience, I play what's called 'adult contemporary' (top hits for middle-aged people who don't follow music much). The volume is down to the just audible level. This allows people to talk to me, but no pressure. Some prefer just to sit and text. I like it best when they are talking on the phone, so I can listen in and guess what's going on. It's a kind of social sudoku. But passengers aren't allowed to play their own music. I'm not going to waste time setting up the Bluetooth or messing with adapters. Plus, I have my own reasons for controlling the audio.

As my conversation with Gerald (let's call him Gerald, he looks like a Gerald) from the back rolls on, I become un-special. He's made the next observation. The one I was waiting for.

'Hey,' Gerald says. 'You look just like that American actress. What's her name? She was in The Great Gatsby…'

'Mia Farrow?' I suggest, but I'm just messing with him. I know who he means.

'Who?'

'Mia Farrow played Daisy. Robert Redford played Jay Gatsby.'

'No, the Leonardo DiCaprio one.'

'Carey Mulligan?' I'm twenty-five. Carey Mulligan is much older than me but looks perpetually twenty-five. I'll take the compliment.

'Yeah, that's her. Carey Mulligan.'

'She's English, not American.' Just for the record, being Carey Mulligan's doppelgänger doesn't make me that different either. A lot of people would pass the actor on the street, none the wiser.

'Really? I thought she was American.'

'She's big in Hollywood. Probably has property in LA,' I say, softening it.

'Probably,' he says.

If people bother to ask, they might be surprised to learn I don't belong to one of those large taxi entities thinking they are going head-to-head with Uber. Taxis competing with Uber is like watching a kitten pounce on a snoozy rottweiler. I might be young. But when it comes to taxi driving, I'm the oldest school of old school. I own my car. I own my taxi licence and plate. I operate solo. And I don't work hard doing it. I don't even give out my mobile number to promote myself like some do, with a stack of semi-gloss business cards at the ready. I just cruise the streets. Some people on the side of the road actually look up from their ride booking app (WiFi can be glitchy in the heart of Australia's largest city), spot my lit-up taxi light and think, 'What the hell. If I just stick out my arm right now...'

'Bluetooth is easy. I'll show you.' The passenger is a girl around my age with short brown hair, no make-up, tatts or piercings. But she did wear a red t-shirt saying, 'Keep Calm and Code.' Meanwhile I'm trying to keep calm while telling her to keep her mitts off my tech. I blocked her lean forward to the front with my arm. The assumption I'm unable to work out a simple Bluetooth connection almost had me pulling over. This one was pushy, wanting her music. Paramore was back, she said. I had to hear it.

'Aren't they a Christian band? I don't have that in my ride,' I say, waiting for the lights to change.

'They aren't a Christian band,' Izzy says (let's call her Izzy, she looks like an Izzy). Her tone went up a few notches. Frustration is like that. 'They're from Tennessee.'

'Being from Tennessee means they are ninety-nine percent likely to be a Christian band.' Finally, green. We move on.

'They're alternative. They won the Grammys,' Izzy's tone almost jumps to 5000 hertz.

'How can you be alternative AND win the Grammys?' I ask, changing lanes. 'That doesn't make sense.'

Dropping down to 100 hertz, Izzy says, 'You're getting a zero-star rating,' before slumping in a sulk.

'On what?' I ask with a chuckle. I had no public engagement listing anywhere. Izzy had nowhere to rate me. Before she thought of taking a photo of my licence display to post on

Instagram, I pull over outside the FUNGO co-working building. At the start of the ride, she told me with a smug grin she works at FUNGO. I knew about FUNGO. It was hard not to know about FUNGO. Their big beard, eco-friendly PR was shameless with their incessant Facebook and Instagram campaigns.

I almost said to Izzy, 'FUNGO? Is that where all the fun goes somewhere else?' Glad I didn't. Otherwise, we wouldn't have had that special crescendo climb over Paramore. It would've been 5000hz all the way.

A friend of mine considered renting a FUNGO space and decided to bring me along for the sales tour. Our FUNGO tour guide forgot to introduce his name and we forgot to ask. But afterward we decided to call him Josh (he looked like a Josh). Josh wore bamboo framed glasses, hemp baseball cap, and a blue t-shirt of a panda with a revolver in each paw. Banksy. Had to admit, I wanted that t-shirt.

'In the early twentieth century, this building was a wool store,' Josh explains, 'then it became a hostel for homeless men. In the nineties, it turned into an engineering firm specialising in hydraulics. Now it's the new way to work - and to live.' He ends with, 'We're a working community,' waving his hand towards a sea of cheap plywood desks, half of them empty. From what I could tell, it was desk space protected by high-end app-based security for people with start-up dreams backed by angel funding. Or non-profits hiding from the public.

Google had influenced the toddleresque interior design, but with a plethora of upcycled fittings (keeping the savings to themselves, the rent was astronomical). What I noticed most was the sound. The acoustics were appalling. Everyone can hear everything, including whoever was playing the pinball machines and ping-pong tables in the 'break space'. The indie acoustic music piped throughout the building couldn't save the sound carnage. To make matters worse (or better), the break space had beer on tap. With drinking alcohol comes raised voices, tones that ricocheted off the concrete floor and the wall's gloss-plastic decor surfaces. If I worked here, I'd be blitzing the bar fridge just to cope. But that's just me. And my friend, it turns out, who told Josh she'd think about it. Which means she wouldn't.

How does a twenty-five-year-old artist own their own taxi plate? As you may have guessed, plates don't cost as much as they used to. Back in 2012, one could take you out four hundred thousand or more. With government subsidies as a financial apology for the legal introduction of ride-share, my father gave me the most unusual of birthday gifts: A taxi plate, licence, and insurance for three years.

Dad was quietly gutted at his only child becoming an artist, imagining me homeless with dental problems, coal dust smudged on my cheeks, speaking in a broad cockney accent. Most parents who find themselves with creative offspring are alike in their horror. Their worry is as predictable as the sun rising. But how can taxi driving be a safe career fallback answer for your young daughter? Still, we had a deal. I was to come up with a Plan B, and he agreed to back it up, as long as my plan was thought through. You should've seen the PowerPoint presentation. My graphics were outstanding. Dad had described my risk assessment as 'Soteria,' which I later learned was the goddess of safety in Greek mythology. My father teaches classics and ancient history at the uni. If anyone needed a career Plan B, it was him. But I don't go there.

Instead, I soak in guilt, as there was one small fact omitted from my risk assessment. Prison.

My mother, a mathematics lecturer at the same university as my father, died of breast cancer a few years ago. It's been just the two of us since. Of course, I miss her. We both do. But Dad was always the more maternal parent. He was the one I went to if I had a problem. Mum was a logician, a little out of reach emotionally speaking. But she would have loved the budget section of my taxi presentation. The bricks and mortar of pitches are the numbers. With mine, I could have built a fortress with turrets. So impressed by my delivery, Dad believed that if my Plan B failed, my Plan C ('C' is for Chaos Rectifier) was corporate report design.

My relief when Izzy finally climbed out of my car was short-lived. Josh of FUNGO, complete with hemp baseball cap, jumps in. He's not wearing the Banksy panda t-shirt though. Today, he has the Batman symbol with Chinese letters running across it. I wasn't going to ask.

'That was lucky,' he says. I thought he was speaking to me, then realised he was on his phone. 'A taxi. I know, retro. Love it.'

'Excuse me?' I whisper. Josh looks at me through his bamboo glasses, puzzled. 'Where do you want to go?' And then he realises. No app, no destination already in the system.

'Get this, she's asking for my address! Wild,' Clearly, Josh and his phone buddy couldn't believe the coolness of it all. 'Yeah, the driver is female.' He looks at me, then says, 'Fuck, she's the spitting image of Carey Mulligan.' I give him a hard stare with my hand out, indicating the need for a destination. He stares back at me, knowing he's seen me before, not just Carey Mulligan. He's trying to place me. I could say 'FUNGO tour', but prefer to let the man paddle. 'Sorry,' Josh says, clocking what I'm waiting for. 'Going to Kurnell National Park. The Visitor Centre.' I type it into my GPS. It was going to be a forty-five-minute drive. Sweet. But then I'd probably end up driving back to the city without a ride. Still, looks like it's about to rain, which could work to my advantage.

Josh continues his phone conversation, giving up on who I am to him. 'I'm meeting an Indigenous artist and some elder for this street art gig we're sponsoring. Fuck knows why we have to schlep out to Kurnell. Anyhoo, I also need a mural for the stairwell at FUNGO. Hoping to squeeze that out of the project somehow…Dunno, something to do with whales, I think.' Josh looks at his smart watch. 'I'm running seriously late, but black fellas are always late, right?' he laughs. Josh spends the rest of the journey boasting about the band he's in. I roll my eyes when he says he plays bass. Which is unkind. Bass is the foundation of a song. Paul McCartney played bass. But let's face it, with young bands, bass is the beginner's guitar.

'Our approach is a blend of Wolfmother and Nick Cave,' he explains, 'but with our own sound.' Jesus. 'We're being approached by some underground venues.' This means poorly run storage cupboards. And here comes the punchline: 'It's not about the money,' Josh says. 'We just want to play our music.' Bloody hell.

Sometimes, when I'm feeling brave, I tell my passengers I'm an artist. Then get them to guess what kind, if they haven't started already.

'Painter?'

'Nope'

'Sculptor?'

'Nope.' Some are spent by then. Others might try 'printmaker'. And if they know their art genres, they offer 'installation'. I shake my head, and they plead with me to cough up. 'When we get there, I'll tell you,' I say before changing the subject. Some forget to ask once I've pulled over, but for those who do, I reply honestly. 'I'm a sound artist.' They look confused. 'What's a sound artist? Like a musician?'

'No, like a visual artist but with sound fed through a speaker or earphones. In galleries, usually, or abandoned spaces.'

Sometimes sound artists use their recordings to create a visual work of art, like the appearance of a sound wave on a piece of paper, which can look like a mountain range, or even a mountain range reflected in water. Sound waves are beautiful. I've been known to collaborate with visual artists to create physical works. But right now, I create solo for legal reasons.

Sound art can really piss people off. In 1952, American composer John Cage organised a public performance by pianist David Tudor, titled *4'33* at Maverick Concert Hall near Woodstock. The pianist sat at the piano, lid closed, for thirty-three seconds (guided by a stopwatch he had activated). After thirty-three seconds had passed, Tudor opened the piano lid and closed it again, then activated the stopwatch to sit silently for another thirty-three seconds. And he did it all one more time. Three movements. Audience members allegedly stormed out. One who remained said at the Q&A afterwards, 'I think we should run these people out of town.' But my thinking is, you can't value sound if you don't value silence. Perhaps that was what Cage was getting at.

Even visual artists can get their knickers in a twist about sound artists. There was a ruckus when Susan Philips won the prestigious UK Turner Prize in 2010 for an audio file. The work was of her singing three versions of a Scottish ballad performed under three different bridges in Glasgow. Philips nabbed £25,000 prize money, a significant sum for most artists. A group of approximately one hundred artists publicly protested outside the Tate Museum, where the award ceremony was being held. The argument was that Philips' work is music, not art. It is with some irony that those attending the award ceremony could not see the protesters but could certainly hear them.

Josh, still on the phone, opens the door and begins sliding out. We are in the Visitor Centre carpark, surrounded by the gentle rustling of trees and bird sounds.

'Excuse me,' I call out, holding up my EFTPOS machine.

'Man, I almost forgot to pay for the ride! Remember when we did that?' he says to his invisible friend. My antiquated workplace systems are an array of nostalgic delights. If I'd said 'Cash only', he would have wet himself. Paying with a wave of his watch, the bass player makes his way towards the Visitor Centre, talking. I wondered if he noticed my watch. But it comes from this century, so probably not. It looks like a standard black Fitbit. Plenty of people have those. I am left-handed, so I wear it on my right wrist out of obvious view.

An old, dark-skinned woman walks from the main doors, heading towards me. She's wearing a bright-coloured floral dress and even brighter cardigan. Josh still doesn't notice and almost knocks her off her feet. 'Hey!' she says, steadying herself.

'Hey!' Josh says back with a smile before entering the building.

I sat watching the woman slowly make her way towards me. I got out, offering to help but she waved down at me, indicating not to bother. 'Want a ride though,' she says. I open the back door for her, and she shuffles in.

'Where to?' I ask.

'Dunno yet,' she says with ease as she opens the back window and breathes in. 'Just go up here and turn left.'

I drive through the forest. We're heading towards the coast, not far away. I don't really know Kurnell, but I can see the area map on my screen.

'It's beautiful here,' I say, deciding to roll my window down too.

The woman nods. 'My Country. Gweagal.'

I don't know what to say to that. 'You must be very proud' doesn't quite cut it. But she has every reason to be. Even I can tell this is a special place, even with asphalt and vehicles driving through it. I then make an assumption and can't help myself. 'Were you supposed to meet a guy from FUNGO at the Visitor Centre? He told me he was a sponsor for an art project involving an Indigenous artist and elder.' It wasn't strictly true. He didn't tell *me* as such. Tomaitos, tomartos.

'Yeah, he didn't come,' she says.

'That was the guy who bumped into you outside,' I say. 'Want me to turn back?

'It's okay,' she waves. 'Time to move on.' I nod. Excellent decision. Nothing is spoken, but as I drive, I watch her expression in the rear-view mirror shift gradually from ease to concern. We've reached the coast. It's hard to enjoy the view, as she's looking back at me, frowning. Following the curve of the coast, we pass a tourist lookout spot for whale watching and a line of carparking spaces. All empty. She's still frowning at me. I drive to the end, which is a helicopter pad.

'We can't go any further. Expecting a chopper to pick you up from here?' I say with a small laugh, an attempt to lighten the atmosphere.

'Park please,' she says. There's tension in her voice.

'I can't park here…'

'The carpark,' she says, gesturing impatiently towards the closest empty space. Feeling like an idiot, I do as I'm told. As soon as we're parked, looking out over the mammoth waves of the South Pacific Ocean, she asks straight up, 'You recording me?' I wished for a helicopter to collect me right then, or an alien spaceship. Anal probes aside, I'd take it. My left hand moves to my watch, and I push a button.

'No,' I say, looking back at her through the mirror, too nervous to turn my body around.

'Not anymore,' she replies, still frowning. The woman is all over me. 'Whatcha doin', girl, recording people in secret?'

'It's for my art…' My hertz level is barely audible to the human ear. But the old lady catches it and bursts out laughing. 'For my art,' she repeats in a sing-song voice that doesn't beckon me to join in. My art project (currently in development) is a sample mix of people's voices as they talk in my cab with traffic sounds as backing. It is a commentary on being in enclosed spaces with strangers. Well, I think it is. Not sure what exactly, but I'm hoping the process is going to tell me. That's the thing about art, you don't feel like you're the one driving.

I figured I could distort the words enough not to get in any trouble, say it was all made up, even. The reality is that the reality is better than anything I could make up. I tried to get people to chat, knowing I was recording. But it never went as well as people not knowing they were being recorded.

'How…how did you know?' I stammer.

'My naughty grandson got one of those watches. Very fancy, aren't they? With voice activation, Bluetooth playback, and that time and date stamping.' Her features rollcall is impressive. She shifts in her seat, gearing up for the main point. 'I told him what I'm gunna tell you. Recording people without their knowledge is wrong.'

'I know, it's against the law…'

'Bugger the law. It's just wrong. How would you like it? Or do you think you're different from other people or something? You think you're special?'

'No….'

'Being an artist doesn't you get some free pass to treat people like this. Just because you're an artist doesn't mean you don't have responsibilities to your community. Responsibly to your community comes first. You treat them with respect. Now get out.'

As I unclip my safety-belt and open the car door, I imagine the old woman getting behind the wheel and driving off just to teach me a lesson. Knowing I had hidden car tracking wasn't a comfort. The woman gets out and walks towards the helipad, beckoning me to follow. Locking the car, I amble after her as she takes a path leading to the rocky ledge.

'Humpbacks migrate south around now,' she says while standing, looking out. We sing them in.' I nod, looking out too, afraid to ask what 'singing in' means. I had a new appreciation of the value of silence. She continues, 'What you reckon it's like being

a whale living underwater? Think it might be hard to see or smell?'
I nod, lips firmly shut. 'Damn right it's hard,' she says. 'Sound is
important for whales to communicate. To survive. And sound
moves fast.' She was right. Sound moves through water four times
faster than air. 'Did you know only five kinds of whales sing?' I
didn't know that. I shook my head. 'Other whales make noises, but
only five whale species sing.' I didn't know the difference between
singing and noises in whale terms, but keep my mouth shut. 'The
difference between singing and noises is that singing has patterns.'
The woman had ESP. Then she sighed. 'Listening to humans isn't
that interesting, girl. There's too much talking as it is.' She had a
point. We have become a species of opinionated prattlers. I can feel
it starting to rain, but we both stay put. 'Now whales…' she says,
'whales are interesting. You want to come out on my boat with my
grandson, the naughty one, and listen, you can,' she says, adding. 'I
got him a hydrophone. Hertz range is point 003 to 250.'

Of course, I nod. As the rain comes down, I don't ever
remember feeling so light. I continue nodding with a maniac's
grin spreading across my face. The woman laughs and nods back.
And then I realise something. Josh from FUNGO changed my life.
I would never have met this woman if it weren't for Josh. And
if it weren't for Izzy, I wouldn't have had Josh leading me to this
woman. I stood staring at the ocean, feeling grateful, so grateful
for Izzy and Josh. In the rain. Which is all I could hear. The rain.

'Come on now,' the woman says, turning back towards the
carpark. 'We're not whales, girl.' I follow, so grateful for this
woman, who will remain nameless. Nameless until she tells me
what it is.

JOINT VENTURE

[Big Donut Cookie]

Chapter One

Sirens were wailing in the background at the time, which I should have seen as a sign. But sirens are part of New York's theme song. With people so close together, there's always going to be trouble. And New Yorkers generally don't look for signs. They just see an opportunity and take it. On that evening, we were sitting in my kitchen, just the two of us, talking over the wail of police cars that faded soon enough. It was a happy moment because she had decided to marry him. She saw the opportunity, and I couldn't blame her one bit. We laughed while eating Chinese take-out from the cardboard boxes, imagining Soph on a pogo stick trying to kiss her six-foot-four groom at the altar. The formal announcement came two days later.

I had a good feeling about it. Dad died six months after Sophia was born, and my older brother had passed away a year after that. Twenty-five years later the family was finally expanding rather than contracting. At least, that's how it looked at the time.

When we were little, I used to sing her name repeatedly. Sophia Lucia, Sophia Lucia. In a taunting way, like brothers are supposed to, along with a sneer so sharp it could cut cables. Immature, I know, and worse, uncreative. But being the older brother, I assumed I had the upper hand. What a mistake. A mistake made over and over and over again. She would backhand with my first two names, plus something extra. Roberto pongo Alfonzo, or Roberto wanna-go Alfonzo, or Roberto can't-grow-a-mo Alfonzo. Can't grow a mo? I was eleven years old, for Christ's sake. Still, I had Italian DNA on my side, and the following year saw black action at my upper lip. First in the class, I might add, but it was a little late to raspberry back at my sister. Soph would have come up with something else anyway. She had a string of them. And pulled out the same standard of rhymed abuse for anyone who tried it on her. She could always hold her own, Sophia Lucia, I'll tell you that.

The heckling continued into adulthood, affection growing with it. We relied on each other. It had been just the two of us for quite some time. The two of us and an ageing mother with no capacity for English or meaningful discourse in any language. On the whole, Ma kept to herself. Due to the language barrier, she sent us off to do the shopping - clothes, food, whatever. It was a lot of responsibility for a couple of kids and opportunity for all sorts of trouble. Except that through her Italian friends, she kept in touch with the prices of goods, making it hard to slip through the net. If we bought the wrong thing we got fried.

The surveillance didn't stop us from one day buying out the local store's supply of Oreo chocolate cookies. Must have been at least twenty packs. We had eaten one pack on the way back home. Creeping up to the house, Ma was right where we wanted her. In front of the television. We hid the rest of the Oreos in our bedroom cupboard, but Ma found them within half a day. The next week, we bought up on mixed candy and hid the stash in the laundry. She found the bag within the hour. A month later, we tried a similar job involving cola bottles. Hiding them under Ma's bed as an attempt at inverse psychology. That night we both got whipped something bad by a fistful of rosaries. It was around that time that Soph and I decided finding secret hiding places was not our area of expertise.

Maternal scrutiny extended as far as the shopping. When it came to receiving real attention, Ma gave daytime television a larger slice of the pie. General Hospital, Days of Our Lives, The Bold and the Beautiful. You name it, she watched it. And had an opinion on everything she saw. The way people dressed, the look in their eyes, the way they walked. She turned off the fluorescents especially, letting the light from the tube work its magic. Sitting on the faux velvet couch against a pattern of purple and brown wallpaper, her eyes shone as she interpreted what was before her. On rare occasions, these refined skills of observation were transferred to life. Even to us sometimes.

As you would expect, there were some ruffles around Sophia's engagement. It wasn't his fault. He was a clover, which I was ready to say when Ma started screaming. We all expected the protest to be about that, about Soph marrying a non-Italian. Maybe that was what was upsetting her deep down. But all we heard was about the poor guy's body language.

'No movement in the hands,' she said, shaking her head. As if it meant anything. 'His eyes look down too much,' she kept saying. As if it was a crime.

Mic loved Soph. You could see it. It's hard to hide that kind of thing. The wedding went ahead, despite my mother's fretful prayers and cries of exasperation. In fact, the day went off without a hitch. The church was nice enough. It was mid-town New York, not too shabby. I had been instructed by Soph to walk as slowly as I could down the aisle before giving her away - playful torture for her husband-to-be. Afterwards, over a hundred people were fed and watered until the small hours in an elegantly decorated hall nearby.

Michael O'Neil. When it came to being a suitor, Mic had some points on the board. In comparison to our family, his background was a tad more financially secure. Boston heritage, not to put too finer point on it. His father had been in banking, then left to become a private developer. Mic's mother hadn't worked since their children were born. They did better than okay.

Tall and broad-shouldered, I bet Mic could have played for the Celtics if he hadn't found the kitchen first. Potatoes were just the beginning. By his early twenties, he was a graduate from some fancy Swiss cooking school and was working around the clock in Manhattan. By mid-twenties, he was a very well-regarded chef in a very well-regarded restaurant, owned by another very well-regarded chef and someone else of a silent nature.

Reputation was all fine and dandy. But by thirty, Mic was itching for his own set-up. And he wouldn't call it 'Mic's' by the way. Mic has too much class for the name-toting bullshit that, admittedly, Italians are famed for. No, he would use an unpronounceable French-sounding word like 'Maquereau' – a word for something quite ordinary, in this case 'mackerel'. I know what mackerel is in French because Mic cooked it for me once, telling me what he was doing every step of the way and getting me to pronounce the name of the dish like a grade-schooler. He had two children with my sister by that stage, maybe that explained it.

'Maquereau grillé, Roberto,' he said while scaling the fish and removing the guts. 'Can you say it?'

'Grilled mackerel,' I replied slowly while making myself a peanut butter sandwich. Despite assumptions about our Italian origins, my family can't cook for shit. Still, I was starving, and Mic took forever to prepare food when he wasn't in the restaurant. He knew I'd still be eating the fish. Although I am only five foot six, I have an appetite that could choke a whale.

'Maquereau grillé,' Mic persevered, though there was a hint of a chuckle. The Irishman would never give up. Quiet persistence was his gig. An admirable quality, particularly when you're on the same side. Even though I was winding him up and he could be a right-royal pain in the arse, we were on the same side, like brothers.

The fish was washed and dried. I did my best Pepe Le Pu accent while rubbing my cheek against his. 'Maquereau grillé' I said at least three times with lips pouted like a sink plug. Sophia walked into the kitchen after putting the kids to bed and snorted at me inelegantly. It was her way of laughing. Elegance wasn't a big part of our early education, and it didn't seem to be rubbing off on us from Mic. He didn't seem to mind. Soph and I were the entertainment.

And he laughed that night while peeling his cheek from mine. He then cut four shallow incisions on each side of the thicker part of the fish. They were lightly sprinkled with flour, brushed with oil, then placed on the fish griller. Cooking the fish was pretty straightforward. The mustard sauce proved to be trickier, however. I can't remember what it was exactly - Mic wrote it down for me somewhere - but it had something to do with butter, cream, shredded onion, English mustard, and a bay leaf. Oh, and cayenne, which I've never had in my cupboard. The sauce took over half an hour to cook and required constant stirring, a killer for the wrist. I couldn't understand why we didn't just squeeze some slices of lemon on the fish and be done with it.

'Maquereau grillé' is as far as my frog language goes, that and 'chérie'. I might throw in the latter on a date if my Italian wiles fail to pull the romantic mood. The former if I'm really desperate. I have been successful in many aspects of my life, but finding a woman who is prepared to sleep full-time on the other side of my queen-size isn't one of them. Some have stayed a matter of months, one for a whole year and a half, but I can't find that person who can get into my way of thinking. I sure as hell can't get into theirs. Ultimately, there are arguments or, worse, the silence that's as loud as a foghorn. Then I'm back to being alone again in my own kind of quiet, which is never as bad.

My Italian is first-class for a Calabrian. Mic learnt the language as best he could for Sophia's sake – and I guess, for the sake of Italian dishes he wanted to experiment with. Ma just kept watching television. She wouldn't speak to him for too long, pretending his textbook Italian was too northern, a different dialect. Soph did her best to explain to Mic that the old woman didn't like conversations with anyone, her own kids included. He blinked a lot at these times. I looked on, hoping Mic wasn't thinking of crying. He didn't, thank Christ. That would be too much – and bait for jokes forevermore.

Like Mic, Soph and I were born in the States. And all three of us were brought up Catholics, though none of us attended church except for special occasions like Easter, Christmas and funerals. But it's hard to break from tradition. While America the Beautiful is all about fresh starts, you are still described as an Italian-American, African-American, Japanese-American,

Irish-American. Even though it's behind you, your ancestry still comes first, whether you like it or not.

One night, just over a year ago, I went over to Soph's. I used to spend quite a bit of time over there. Not just for uncle duties, but because Mic was always tied up at the restaurant and Soph could use the company. She tried to get me to help her with laundry and cleaning, but I put a stop to that before it even started. I may be a lot of things, but I'm not a putz. Organising toys was as far as I was prepared to go. She knew, on the sly, I enjoyed doing it.

So, I walked through the front door, and the girls ran to me from across the lounge room to jump on my shoulders, as they were prone to do. I love them to bits and hope they never grow taller than me. Lucy (or Lucia, depending on which house you're sitting in) was seven and Gabriel (ending with an 'la', again, when culturally required) was five. Lucy is dark and a little on the quiet side, while Gab, stocky and fair-headed, has more chutzpah than a Colombian coke dealer.

There was still some time before bed, so we played the new Harry Potter video game. Talk about milk a franchise. Well, the girls played. I clicked the mouse all over the screen, trying to activate something, anything. Gab did her best to guide me, but I was tired and frustrated, so they finally agreed to shut down and hear a story from that most ancient of possessions, a book. I could handle that.

The story was about some Irish kid whose parents had split up. Halfway through, I looked back at the front inside cover to find an inscription of best wishes from Mic's mother to the girls. The story continued in a raw fashion of emotional turmoil and financial challenges. Whatever happened to pirates and dragons, I asked. The girls shook their heads and urged me to keep reading. I continued, but wondered how long it would take for the IRA to blow the little boy's arms off. Fortunately, it didn't come to that. Instead, the ending saw the sudden appearance of a lovable long-lost godmother with ample breasts. I found it unconvincing, but the audience seemed satisfied when I bedded them down, distributed kisses and switched off lamps.

Soph was washing the dishes. I decided to let them drain, sitting down in front of the television instead. She joined me soon after, talking about Mic starting his own restaurant. I was watching basketball, the Knicks playing the Lakers at home. Seeing where it was heading, I gave in and turned on the mute. My right eye looked at my sister while the left kept score.

The topic wasn't a new one. It was inevitable that Mic would have his own place one day, but I worried about Soph's assumption it would eventually see Mic at home more. Apparently, once the business was established and the staff knew what they were doing, he could adjourn. That was her angle. The theory never added up to me. People running their own businesses generally tend to have trouble breathing off-premises.

I'm a payroll worker, a journalist for NYC Magazine. It's the easy-read version of The New Yorker. And I was the easiest read of them all. Early on, my editor said I was good with the feel-goods. This was not a compliment. It was a curse. Nothing with edge would appear under my byline as long as Artie was at the helm, and he ran the place like it was his own business. He never left, not even for a decent cup of coffee. But, over time, I realised that, for a journalist, I am highly unambitious. Feel-goods and What's On columns, my staple, meant I got paid a regular wage with regular hours, like an office worker. While others were working nights and weekends on crime and tragedy – always happening, it seemed, out of hours – I could go on dates, visit my family and go see baseball and basketball games without interruption. Sometimes I even got free tickets.

On the odd occasion, Soph would ask Mic to give up the food business and become a soft-hitting journo like her brother. It was meant in jest, but we all knew there was something behind it. She wanted Mic home. I just wish she'd say stuff like that when I wasn't around. Even though he smiled, Mic couldn't look at me at times like that.

Sitting on the couch, the Knicks dropped back by four. Soph was still on the restaurant thing, and then an idea sprang into my mind.

'There's a restaurant on the Lower East Side, on Houston, that closed recently. I used to go there – old Jewish kosher. Damn shame. I liked the pickles.' Looking at the television, I noticed we were now behind by two with twenty seconds on the clock. The coach was about to have a seizure.

'Lower East Side property is getting more expensive by the day,' Soph said.

I kept my focus on the screen but nodded, 'Which is why maybe Mic should look into it sooner rather than later.' Soph squeezed my shoulder til it hurt. I could tell her face was lit up, but I wasn't watching. Anderson had just intercepted the ball and shot a miracle three-pointer from outside. We made it back, winning by one at the sound of the horn.

Chapter Two

The next day, I was walking Mic down Houston. Traffic was jammed as usual. With the Williamsburg Bridge not far away, parking would be impossible. 'But who parks in New York?' I asked. Mic nodded, looking even more earnest than normal as we approached what had been Noah's Deli. He liked the brownstone building and the location. I pointed out that we were close to Alphabet City. Tagged after it's unadventurous road names–Avenue A, Avenue B, Avenue C, etc. –historically, Alphabet City had been a pocket of bad juju. A far cry from Sesame Street. But over the years, crime in the area had dropped rapidly. Property-renovating yuppies had 'discovered it' and were, as always, a force to be reckoned with. Alphabet City's low-income residents - lawbreakers and hard-working innocents - had been forced off Manhattan, joining the bridge-and-tunnels in suburbs like Brooklyn, where we all grew up and where my mother still lives. I live in Brooklyn too, in a one-bedroom bachelor apartment, which sounds more exciting than it is.

At three o'clock the next day, we followed the real estate agent inside. It was during Mic's mid-afternoon break. Sophia came along, leaving the kids to be picked up by a friend. Walking around the kitchen, Mic nodded as if his head was on a loose spring. He was excited, as was my sister. She was speaking quickly in Italian to herself. Her husband didn't understand a word, but he was in his own world anyway. Potential floated in the air and settled like the dust we breathed and touched at every turn. The place had been closed for a month, but the listing surfaced at the agency only two days prior. It was still fresh.

While giving murmurs of support, I assumed Mic's Dad-The-Developer would be making the dream a reality, that a trip from Boston would be next on the list. I was right. Mr O'Neil inspected the property early the next week along with a small troop of building, financial and legal advisors. The seller was holding out for someone to buy the entire building, not just the restaurant. Mr O'Neil decided it was a worthwhile investment. Only one nod was required from him.

The deal was looking good until lunch that Sunday. I was eating with Soph, Mic and the girls at their place. Mic's dad had called the night before, explaining he was caught up in the courts over a development in Philadelphia. Funds were temporarily frozen, so he didn't have the ready cash to pay the deposit, but it would be available in a couple of months, maybe three. He could guarantee that. This sort of thing happens all the time, he said.

'Some people try to screw you in court. It's a business in itself,' he explained to Mic. But O'Neil had good representation. 'It'll be fine,' he had said. 'The money will thaw.' And what's not to believe? Money moved around that man like neurons and electrons. No one could see the dollars, but they were there.

According to the real estate agent, there was some serious interest expressed in the building from a Japanese firm and some Texans. Normally, I don't believe a syllable from property pimps, but we were looking at a prime site, and we all knew it. The situation looked grim. Over lunch, Mic shrugged his shoulders and focused on what was on the plate before him. Gab, who was sitting next to me, started to wail. The artichoke salad with marinated lamb wasn't cutting it, as far as she was concerned. Mic chewed on his food, his mind elsewhere, probably the brownstone on Houston. I grabbed a couple of slices of bread from the basket and made up a lettuce, tomato and sliced lamb sandwich. Lucy asked if she could have the same. I checked for authorization and Soph nodded. The youth of today, it's all about presentation.

That night I had a dream. Soph was looking at me across a table. Or was it a school desk? I remember Ma was there, then she walked out of the room. Actually, I think it was a community hall. Anyway, Soph didn't have the Roberto-can't-grow-a-mo look. It was more UNICEF donation advertising. Help us now, and you'll stop feeling guilty – that guilt you didn't even know was there until that instant. I woke up in a sweat.

The family didn't know it, but I had the money. Not to buy the whole building, but for the deposit - and a bit extra if Mic needed it for some mortgage payments and a renovation kick-off. Feel-good journalists don't earn that kind of bread. The money came from elsewhere. Sounds like the beginning of a joke, but a man walked into a bar. He happened to be a retired financial advisor, and I happened to be sitting on the stool next to him. We were both drinking Corona in spite of pandemic word associations (No, beer sales didn't drop. I did the research and wrote an article on it), guessing how the Super Bowl was going to shape up that season.

To be honest, I find it increasingly difficult to meet new people socially. Not just women but men, too. Making friends seems to be something you do until your mid-twenties. After that, you're on your own. Bars are getting noisier, making it harder to throw in a casual line. Rather than football games, screens are more likely to have music video clips and reality shows - both on mute, with some other music blaring. So when

I found the old-style bar with old-style customers like Pete, I made the most of it. It wasn't a place to meet women, which probably made my time there all the more relaxing.

Although Pete was retired, he still had his finger on the pulse. I had experienced my fair share of conversations with Wall Street jocks, usually crouched down talking to them through their Audi passenger windows, trying to make some sense of the market. And wondering, of course, where on earth they park. But Pete had some simple tips I could get my head around. I signed up with a broker and followed through. Over beers and ball seasons, my profits built. Slowly. He advised taking some out, putting it into a long-term savings account. A buffer.

'Everyone needs a buffer,' Pete would say. 'Don't ever get cocky, Bob.'

He called me Bob. If anyone else called me Bob, I would've clocked them immediately. From Pete, it was alright. The pandemic, in its thickest, made the downturn more than just about money. 'It's different from the GFC,' said Pete, 'but in some ways the same.' It still left many eating dust. Then there was the usual build-up of hope, then ambition. Some punters crashed, some bought low big time. Pete and I kept playing steadily. I did what I was told and generally came up even, if not on top. Then one night, the night the Yankees were in the semi-finals, Pete wasn't on his usual stool. He wasn't anywhere. I asked Kahlil, the barman, but Pete hadn't been seen for a couple of weeks.

Turned out Pete had a stroke. When tracking him down at the hospital, I finally met his wife, Kate. She seemed like a decent person, the sort of woman who had a generous heart but was no pushover. I hoped that Pete had good times with her when he wasn't at the bar talking to me.

Pete woke with half his body paralysed. The doctors predicted more movement in future, given intensive physio treatment. I visited him on a semi-regular basis at the hospital and then at his apartment. Kate seemed happy about my appearances. Though he had trouble speaking and couldn't drink alcohol, we watched some games and continued our routine as best we could. As you would expect, Pete's market tips were nonexistent. I sat with what I had in the hope that it was the right thing to do. Eventually, Pete said, 'Hold them, Bob.' They were his first whole words spoken to me in months, and I was grateful. At home that night, I wondered if he was talking about the shares, or maybe it was about holding onto family or friends, or bottles of beer. On the next visit I clarified the point.

'Pete, when you said hold them, you were talking about the shares, right?'

'Right,' he said, then added, 'What the fuck else would it be about?' His speech had certainly improved at a rapid rate. Kate, who was shifting his pillow at the time, laughed, then asked if I wanted a coffee. Things were looking up. The next week, a second stroke sent Pete into a coma. It happened at four o'clock on a Tuesday afternoon. It may as well have been the darkest hour of the night, that time when the crime and tragedy journalists take their notes. He died two weeks later. I had a few beers for Pete at the bar that night, more than a few. But it was in his name, and I knew he would have understood. Later that week, I sold a quarter of my shares, transferring the money into my savings account and held the rest. I didn't really know what I was doing, but the movement released an air of stagnancy.

By the time it came round to surveying my finances for the restaurant deal, my buffer looked substantial. If I sold the rest and combined the lot, I could help Mic out of the hole. I worked out that I could be a real player, forty percent of the project. Which meant ultimately earning forty percent of the profits once the apartments above the restaurant were sold. Mic could buy me out of the 'Maquereau' share when he was ready. Pete had always urged me to look into property. I decided to go for a walk, mull it over. I passed bookstores, delis, a pet grooming salon, apartment blocks, an art gallery and restaurants all in full operation. Returning home, I still felt good about it.

You can't tell an Italian that mixing business with pleasure is a bad idea because we do it all the time. And family business is what our history has been all about. If disagreements and confrontation are what give people the jeebies, it's important to note that Italian families yell at each other even when nothing's wrong.

I went in and cranked up the project. Upon first hearing the news, Mic looked like he was about to hyperventilate with excitement, and Sophia wasn't far behind. We were to form one company, Mic, his dad and me. Sounded sensible, tidy. Mr O'Neil apologised over the phone that he couldn't participate financially for a couple of months, but will make up for it then. The Philadelphia case was going as expected. He gave me an outline of how the project would progress. Both the apartments and the restaurant needed some considerable building work to adhere to council requirements and for the ultimate goal of creating profit. Fortunately, most of the building was already empty, and the rest had already received notice from the previous owner, who had originally intended to do the overhaul himself. Something had changed that.

A construction loan was needed, which O'Neil would sort out when the time was right. I would be paying forty percent of expenses. When fluid, O'Neil would pay me sixty percent of the deposit, taxes, insurance, bank fees and any mortgage repayments I make on my own. Once paid, my extra money would be transferred to cover forty percent of the construction costs. He talked about local architects and builders he had already used on other occasions in New York. He also mentioned some solid contacts in council who could help streamline approval. At every point, he asked me if it sounded okay. It did. It sounded great.

I had eaten with O'Neil a couple of times before the settlement. Saw how Luce and Gab ran around his long legs and how Soph gave him a big hug when he arrived. I had already heard much about the family, about trips to Boston with the girls. Soph always had nice things to say about them. More than polite, she really meant it. They were the second family she had hoped for, the one with relatives who were alive and could pull themselves away from the television. I didn't feel bad about that. I was happy for her and probably subconsciously just wanted a piece of that family feeling for myself.

When it came to the brownstone on Houston, some decisions had to be made. I preferred sending emails, easier for three-way communication. Mic had to get into the habit. O'Neil always answered but was brief, which was the sign of a busy man who had done this a thousand times before. He called me on occasion to explain some finer points. Mic deferred to the old man a lot, which you would expect. I guess I did too. Once the purchase was settled, Mic and I bought a special bottle of Krug champagne and went back to his place to celebrate with Soph.

The girls were picking up the vibe and were excited too, though still not fully understanding what the fuss was about. We lit candles while Mic carved and distributed a spice-rubbed turkey with fruit and nut filling that somehow tingled and melted in your mouth simultaneously. It was like an early Thanksgiving. Holding my glass, I paid silent homage to Pete while Gab crawled under the table to play with her dad's shoelaces.

As agreed by all concerned, I continued to make the monthly payments until O'Neil was ready to join in. All angles were considered. If disaster struck, another backer wouldn't be hard to find. Alternatively, we could sell up, still making some money, though nowhere near as much if we hung in there. The property market was healthier than it had been in years. Further escalation was to be expected. Getting in on the game was on everyone's lips. Any way I looked at it, we couldn't lose.

Chapter Three

A couple of months later, I was at the office, cornered by Artie over a story about the Cloisters Museum. Vandals had got in and ripped up some of the courtyard plants, herbs mostly. Not exactly front-page news. The Metropolitan, which ran the museum, had already gathered a group from Harlem to assist in replanting. It was a community project, a feel-good. And I was feeling good that day. So good, I told Artie about the brownstone project. He nodded and said the real estate in that area was first-class. He then asked, 'You're an investor?'

'Yep,' I said with a grin.

'You've got a joint venture contract, right?'

'Joint venture contract?' I asked.

'With the others,' he said. 'If you don't, you'd better do it now.'

'They're family, Artie.' I said, eyes dropping to stare at the floor.

'Even more reason.' His laugh was dipped in acid. 'Believe me. Family think they can get away with anything. Why? Because they are family.' I looked at Artie sideways, wondering what his family did to him. Poor guy.

'I'm not worried,' I shrugged. 'We've got a stack of emails all about it.'

Looking up again, Artie had an expression I knew well. *If you don't do it, you're a halfwit who doesn't deserve a job at McDonalds, let alone one at NYC magazine.* He added with, 'Are you going uptown, then?' The expression had been maintained. I was on my way.

The last time I visited the Cloisters was on a clear, crisp spring day about five years ago to impress a date with my cultural knowledge. That is, the cultural knowledge I'd gleaned from trawling the net the day before. Today, I remember significantly more about the Cloisters than the woman, which says something. Leaving the office, I also remembered there were two public routes to get there. The turtle approach involved taking the M4 Madison Avenue bus, journeying from high-priced boutique stores through the lower-rent neighbourhoods of Harlem and Washington Heights. Tourists loved this ride, watching it all from behind the safety glass. But, like my previous visit, I took the hare approach, hopping on the subway via the A line. Much faster. Whichever way you go, the destination was something else again.

You feel protected in the Cloisters. That's what cloisters were originally designed to do: protect monks from the workers. That is, from real life. A monastic cloister is usually a rectangular building (from above, it's like a picture frame) surrounding a garden (the picture within the frame). A covered walkway runs between the garden and the buildings (like the cardboard mount between the frame and the picture itself). Imagine collecting four different medieval European cloisters from France and reassembling them together in Manhattan. That's what sculptor and architecture enthusiast George Bernard did in the early nineteenth century. My country is excellent at taking bits and pieces from elsewhere and throwing them all together to make it bigger and, in our view, better. It's easy to be cynical about this process of building a nation, but when you get to the Cloisters, all you feel like doing is smiling and breathing.

Perched on a hill, the monastic setting overlooks the Hudson River. As history would expect, John D. Rockefeller got involved. In 1924, he bought Bernard's cloisters and associated medieval art and artefact collection, then threw in his own medieval collection and offered it all to the Metropolitan Museum of Art as a donation. They, of course, accepted. Snap.

Being a New Yorker, I can choose what to pay for entry. My media pass got me in for free, but I paid a donation anyway. Security was an old guy who had a nametag that read 'Martin Kersnovske'. If pressed into a jog, Martin would possibly have a heart attack. But he could pick up a phone to call administration, which he did for me, tracking down the public relations officer who I'd talked to as I was leaving Artie and his attitude. There seemed to be some holdup, so I gestured towards the nearby garden area. Staring at me, Martin shook his head authoritatively while still listening to the earpiece. I nodded in thanks, as if misinterpreting, and made my way.

Wandering through the courtyard gardens, I took a small number of photographs. The damage was more extensive than expected. Most of the plants had been pulled out of the ground and thrown across the cobble-stoned arcades. The trunks of small trees had been badly bent if not broken in half. Everything green looked ripped up or jumped on or both. It was hard to imagine the minds behind the massacre, but I guessed they would be hard pressed winning a point on Jeopardy. The museum itself hadn't been touched. That might have been next if security hadn't turned up in time. I figured Martin wasn't one of them.

The magazine would usually send someone for pics, but I'd taken a photography course a few years back, and my shots had satisfied the artwork department enough in the past. It made me a two-for-one as far as staffing went. They preferred to keep their best and finest photographers for the hard stories anyway.

I watched the youth volunteers doing their best to pull nature back together and introduced myself to a woman, a grown-up, wearing a scarf wrapped around her head. Before approaching, she was shielding her eyes in the sun and pointing with a gardener's glove, directing members of the team to various areas in need.

'Hi,' she replied, though still somewhat distracted. After repeating my introduction, I asked for some information about the garden. She looked straight at me for the first time and repeated, 'NYC Magazine?'

'That's right.'

'I'm not supposed to talk to the media, sorry.' She did look genuine in her apology, which is rare in my journalism experience. 'There's a woman by the name of Carolyn Dickson… from the museum…'

'I think she's making her way any minute now,' I said. 'And you are?'

'Gerry.' She took her hand out of her glove and shook mine. Not too hard, not too soft, but still a little dirty. She looked in her early maybe mid-thirties, around my age. Regardless of the wide-brimmed straw hat in her left hand, her face had experienced a fair share of the elements. I don't see women looking like that too often. It was nice.

'So you're responsible for the reconstruction of the vandal damage?' I asked.

'Responsible? No, I'm just assisting as part of the community project.'

'You look like you know more than anyone else here.'

'I'm a gardener for the city, usually in Central Park. Thought I could take some time out to help these people.'

'Help out the Met?'

'Help the community project.' The tone could have been terse, but she seemed relaxed and just a little distracted by her worker bees.

'Ah, right. Thanks for your time,' I said.

Carolyn Dickson walked over the centuries-old cobblestones as fast as her high-heeled shoes could carry her. Extending a clean hand with polished nails, she said, 'Hi, I'm Carolyn. You must be Roberto from New York magazine.' I nodded and released her firm grip. 'Thanks for coming, Roberto. I see you've met Gerry, our horticulture hero. Naturally, we have our own gardeners, but as you can see, the damage is significant. We decided to turn this tragedy into an opportunity for positive community involvement.' Carolyn flashed her salt-white teeth, clearly expecting something from me after her short but focused PR pitch.

'Fabulous,' I said, but had trouble feeling it. Gerry smiled and pointed to where she was escaping. I watched her walk off. It was a sad but understandable betrayal.

Carolyn continued, 'It's important for you to know that these are special gardens. More than 250 species of plants were sourced, similar to those grown during the Middle Ages, including medicinal herbs. The design was drawn according to horticultural information found in medieval treatises, poetry, and medieval works of art.'

'So the plants relate to some of the art you have?'

'Some, yes. We are standing in the Unicorn Garden. The plants here depict what appears in the Unicorn tapestries inside.'

'Unicorns being mythical.'

'Yes,' Carolyn replied, her expression a version of Artie's 'you're a half-wit'. Sometimes it pays not to think aloud, but it was too late, so I elaborated.

'If the Unicorn is mythical, then this courtyard garden is a fantasy-turned-reality. Quite a beautiful achievement.'

'Was reality...' Carolyn said with doubt lingering, almost human.

'And will be again in no time,' I said, turning to the crouched youth nearby. 'Look at them go.' Now I was doing the pitching. Carolyn began to look more relaxed. We discussed the community project further. After jotting down names of plant donors, I took some more shots guided securely by the hand of Carolyn. Turning to her, I asked, 'Once the courtyard gardens are replanted, kids could still come and play around here, can't they?'

'Oh, yes, absolutely. Admission is free for children. Our education department devises all sorts of wonderful activities both for schools and families. I can find you a program flyer if you like.'

'That would be wonderful.'

'Now?'

'Now would be wonderful.'

I made my way over to Gerry and asked to take her photo. She obliged with the gentlest of smiles. It was important that I had her last name for the caption. At least that was what I told her. As if on cue, Carolyn was clicking her heels towards me while flapping a brochure. I took it with thanks and skimmed the pages, thinking of Gab and Luce running around the cloister columns and shrieking. Sundays would be best. According to the brochure that was Family Day. I bid my adieu to both Gerry and Carolyn and decided to take the bus back to the office. The scenic route.

'I'm ringing about the joint venture contract.'

'The what?' Mic asked.

'The joint venture contract,' I repeated.

'With the bank?'

'No, between the three of us – you, me and your dad,' I said. 'We don't have one yet, but we need it. Just so that we know what's what.'

'Okay,' he replied. 'I'll talk to Dad about it.'

'I emailed you both about it a couple of weeks ago, explaining the whole thing. Did you receive it?'

'Sorry, Roberto, I probably did. Things have been crazy at work.'

'Should I call your dad?'

'No, it's okay. Leave it with me.'

So I did. And time rolled on, gathering moss with it. O'Neil seemed permanently away from all telephones and unable to pick one up. Weeks went by. I knew that O'Neil's frozen finance had thawed because action was happening on site. I had not been notified. My emails were being ignored. A feeling of unease descended. I attempted talking to Soph about it, but she made it plain that the project was between me, Mic and the grand Poo-Bah. Not her. The separation was out of character. She usually got involved in everything. But I suspected there was some thought behind it. Soph was being sensible, applying the 'too many cooks' principle.

I tried concentrating on positive things, like Gerry, for instance. Who was positive in my head at least. The Cloisters article was published without editing, though Gerry's photo didn't make it. I'd conducted some light research on Google to make contact and ask her out for a drink. But she was hiding under a digital bush somewhere. I wandered through Central Park, averaging three times a week, discovering areas I'd never been before. Being 840 acres of nooks and crannies, maybe it's not so surprising. At one point, I called the Cloisters, but the garden project had finished. I tracked down the Harlem Community Centre, but no one was willing to give a number. Not even to a journalist, or maybe it was because I was a journalist. I was about to leave a message at Parks and Land Development, a branch of the City Council, but lost my nerve at the last minute. While I'm no rat pack crooner, I don't usually lose my nerve over calling a woman. However, this wasn't any ordinary woman. This was a woman with bashed-up boots and hands like my grandmother's. She had me round her little, but gardening-strong, finger. As I slumped back in my office chair, it dawned on me. I was mulch.

Gerry, I thought while sitting on the lounge next to my mother, watching television. This could possibly be considered inappropriate, but Ma never showed much interest in what I was thinking anyway. Instead, she was locked onto reruns of 'Everyone Loves Raymond'. Except she didn't love Raymond, she hated him. The wife came out a little better but not by much. The old guy was her favourite. I had an intense disinterest in all of them, but watched it anyway. Well, I pretended to.

Thinking about Gerry was just enhancing my frustration, so I decided to ponder on something else. My mind drifted back to the project, my other default of gnawing uncertainty. The two most engaging things in my life were Gerry and the project. Both were new to me, foreign, and I didn't have any real contact with either of them. It was like playing ping-pong alone without a bat.

I reflected on the day we first settled the Houston brownstone, just before the champagne and spice-rubbed turkey. The seller had already made an extension and our backs were against the deadline. We had to purchase that afternoon, otherwise we would lose the deal. Mic and I sat in a solicitor's office. O'Neil's voice was disembodied from a conference phone. It was saying that the settlement of the property should be in his company's name for now.

'Why is that, Mr O'Neil?' I had asked, surprised. 'What about our own company, the one we formed altogether?'

'Because I'm organising the construction loan and the bank has requested both loans to be in my company's name.' He paused. 'Don't worry, kid. We'll sort it out. You're a vital part of the project, forty percent.'

It was the first time in fifteen years anyone had called me kid. But considering how I was feeling it was probably accurate. The solicitor was costing us three hundred bucks an hour. My contemplation time was kept to a minimum. O'Neil continued to discuss the game plan in detail, ensuring that I understood what he was saying, and that I felt comfortable. We all ultimately gave the nod, signed the deal, and walked out. The property was all in his company's name. Using my money.

I'd paid the deposit, taxes, fees, and three-monthly mortgage payments since. The rest of my finances had been sunk in the construction. And now O'Neil was dodging me. Mic was also hard to find, more than usual. On the odd occasion I managed to catch him, he was vague though still appearing earnest.

Mic wouldn't screw me. No way. I told myself. *They're all just busy.* While sitting on the couch next to my muted mother, the bad feeling, the one I'd kept at bay, was slowly wrapping itself around me like a psychopathic octopus. Then the possibilities came hurtling out from the dark end of the spectrum towards me like missiles. It was possible that O'Neil could be elusive for quite some time. It was possible I had been made the largest fool in development history. It was possible that I had, in fact, lost everything. And then my mother laughed.

Chapter Four

The next morning, I felt foolish. Night allows paranoia to get a good, strong foothold and swing right into the saddle of your psyche. It can remind you of all the things you can't see, you don't know, you aren't in control of. It can remind you that you don't hold the reins. Vulnerability seeps through your pores and soaks into your dreams. With sun now streaming through the window, I rose from my bed and scratched my butt cheek. The humdrum of daily ritual had never appeared more attractive. I moved through the paces. Shower, shave, breakfast, teeth, traffic, office, coffee, turn on computer, check emails.

Scanning down the inbox list of about twenty messages, O'Neil's was sitting close to the end. I bee-lined to it and double-clicked. Expecting a confirmation that all was fine and dandy, the message was a request from both O'Neil and Mic to cease my request for a joint venture contract. My efforts in sourcing the property have been appreciated, but further assistance as 'advisor to the project' was no longer required. There was no mention of monies owing, nothing about my property deposit, taxes, fees or payments. No reference to my forty percent.

They are trying to screw me. And at that point, I felt my whole family fall away from me. I was alone, except Ma. No, I really was alone.

Before I had time to cry or beat my keyboard into plastic chips, Artie was moving fast towards my cubicle. It looked like he had downed three coffees already. Mine remained unsipped. My stomach was paradoxically churning, but also like lead.

'You - in my office,' Artie barked. 'Now.' He swivelled like a Latino dancer back in the direction he came. The man was pushing sixty-five, overworked and, taking diet into account, suffered mildly from malnutrition. How he managed to move so nimbly was beyond comprehension. I followed behind dutifully, unable to imitate the choreography. I hadn't even sat down on the opposite side of Artie's desk when he started talking.

'I'm getting heat from the boss,' he said. This was a first. Artie getting heat from anyone was unheard of. The man was constantly on fire. *'You work for someone?'* was on my lips, but he was on a roll. 'They're wanting more.'

'More?'

'Readership is slipping. The people need something to wet their pants about.' I nodded, not understanding. Artie continued. 'They're after edge, crisis, call it what you will.'

'Tragedy.'

Artie snapped his fingers and pointed at me. 'That's right, tragedy. But tragedy in the works. It must be active.'

'Active tragedy,' I confirmed, trying my best not to throw up from my personal active tragedy.

'The thing is, Roberto, this isn't really your gig. Let's face it, you're a feel-good.' I glowered at him from my seat. He either didn't catch it or wasn't interested. 'You can have a go, but...' While the sentiment was soft, his face still had that *If you don't do it, you're a halfwit who doesn't deserve a job at McDonalds.*

'I need it by Monday week. And I need to know what you are doing leading up to delivery. You've got to check in, Roberto.'

A sigh released from my lips. 'And what if I fail to match the task, Artie?'

'You're on half-time, half pay,' he said and then grinned. 'Which is probably fine. You're about to make a ton on that property, right?'

When in training for journalism, they say do your research, check your facts. And checking the facts generally means going straight to the source. Doesn't matter how high in the corporate ladder or government offices you need to shoot, if the story sits there, you go for it. You've got to play by the rules, don't be aggressive and don't do anything that may be perceived beyond the law. But go to the source. That's number one.

The first thing I did after coming out of Artie's office was hail a cab and head to Sophia's. She wasn't the source, and I'm no great journalist. But she was my sister and I thought I could straighten out the story at least. Perhaps find out that I had misinterpreted the email before buying a gun and taking the next train to Boston. She was home but was unable to let me in. 'We're on our way out,' she said. Gab was squeezing past to give me a hug, but was intercepted by her mother's hand.

'Gab, go wash your face and get your coat, we're running late.'

Gab asked, 'Where are we going?'

'I told you to go wash your face.' Turning back to me she said, 'Sorry Roberto, gotta fly.'

'Can I come round tonight? I've got to talk to you. It's urgent.'

'Tonight's not good.'

'We need to talk, Soph.'

'Look, if it's about this project thing, I don't want to hear about it.'

'They're saying I'm not even a part of it, yet all my money is in there. It's under their name.'

'I said I don't want to talk about it.'

At that, the door was closed. I waited twenty minutes outside her building, but they didn't emerge. Maybe they were going out, maybe they weren't. Everything looked questionable. I took another cab, heading across town through Central Park. If Gerry was there, I didn't see her. Joe Public was everywhere, however. Walking, jogging, riding horses, skateboarding, rollerblading, buying hot dogs and pretzels, lying on the grass. They didn't understand. It had no right to be such a beautiful day.

Arriving at Mic's current place of work, I paid the driver. Already conscious of what I might not be able to afford, he only scored a minimum tip. It was early. The restaurant wasn't open yet, but a waiter was watering the two neatly pruned pot plants flanking the entry. I walked past, through the door, then kept walking like I owned the joint. The maître d' followed behind, explaining they weren't open and asking how she may assist, then requesting I not enter the kitchen. 'Sir, please. That's not public access.'

Mic was coming out of the cool room. By way of expressing my current mood, I grabbed the nearest saucepan and slammed it on the bench. It was a move I saw in a film recently. It had been successful in hastening the plot. Unfortunately, the pan had some boiling hot oil in it, which splattered on my hand and arm. With gritted teeth, I decided to deal with the pain later.

'Roberto,' Mic said. He looked wary and kept his distance, the way most would when confronted with a crazy person. 'How are you doing?'

'Very angry,' I replied. 'And you?'

The maître d' decided to interject with authority. 'Sir, I'm going to have to ask you to leave.' I slammed the saucepan again. The oil didn't hurt as much the second time around.

'It's okay. People slam saucepans here all the time,' Mic said quietly. His hands slowly raised as if I was pointing a gun at him. If the gesture was a way of calming me, it didn't work.

'What's with the email, Mic? What about my fucking forty percent?' I turned to the staff and said through gritted teeth, 'Pardon my French.'

'Roberto, if you continue in this way, Chérie is going to have to call the police,' Mic nodded towards the maître d'.

I turned to the woman behind me. 'Your name's, Chérie?' I asked.

'Yes, it is.' Venturing into negotiation mode, she asked in turn, 'And yours is?'

'Pepé Le Pew.' I tried the glower and, unlike with Artie, it had a response. Chérie walked slowly out of the kitchen and made her way to the lamp-lit mahogany desk to make a call. Hello officer.

'You better go, Roberto,' Mic said. 'We'll talk about this later.'

I had to agree. By this time, my hand felt like it was being fried for a burger. Releasing my grip from the saucepan, I walked towards my brother-in-law and gripped his upper arm with my good hand.

'Sooner, Mic,' I said. 'Much sooner than later.' At that, I walked out with the same determination as my entry and with all the dignity of a turd in the middle of a driveway.

For an Italian, it's not often that I lose my cool. That was the problem. I was out of practise. If applied well, anger can leverage what you want. On that day, I had nothing. The following day, I had even less. Mic had served a restraining order against me, a temporary Order of Protection, courtesy of the Family Court. The cop was at my door bright and early with the paperwork, proving legal bureaucracy can be speedy but only when it's working against you.

'You're not to go near Sophia, her husband or their kids,' he said. 'Do you understand?'

'My sister? My nieces?' I asked. My family.

'That's the drill. That means their home, workplaces, schools and day care. No phone calls, letters or messages through other people.'

'On what grounds?'

'Aggravated harassment, disorderly conduct and stalking.'

'Stalking?'

'You've been hanging around outside their apartment building,' he replied. 'Their doorman's a witness.'

'That was once. I thought she was coming down. I wanted to ask her something.'

'Not my problem. You get your day in court in a month's time. Here's your summons for the court hearing,' the officer fingered the form. 'Violation of this Order of Protection may see you arrested. Get my drift?'

The idea seemed surreal, then turned to insanity when recalling Gabby's birthday was the following Friday. Her party was to be held after school at the park near the zoo, but now it would be impossible to attend. I had never missed one of the girls' birthdays. Mic had, due to work commitments, but I hadn't. *How could Soph let this happen?* I asked myself over and over. But she had. Her signature was alongside Mic's on the form. It was all there in black and white.

The doctor had checked my numbing hand and lower arm straight after the restaurant visit.

'Nasty,' she said while examining the blistering and weeping cooking oil burns. I was feeling nauseous more than anything. She gave it some salve, wrapped it in a plastic bandage and recommended that I give it a rest for a couple of days. I explained that I was a journalist, that I needed the hand to type. She explained that she was a doctor and that her credentials beat mine. Nonetheless, I was back on my laptop at home as soon as I returned home. An email was sent to O'Neil demanding fairness. I was brief. Two sentences, in fact. Leaving the 'I haven't had time to read it' excuse out of the equation. There was no response, so I sent the same email the next day. Nothing.

A surprise trip to Boston became inevitable. The restraining order didn't cover Mic's father. I decided to go unarmed, not that I've ever owned a gun. Not that I ever thought I'd want to own one. Events, or rather the lack of them, reminded me to be open-minded. I was unarmed, with a sore arm hidden by my corporate sleeve. I was wearing my suit. One of those blue ones that are in fashion, brighter than navy. Soph had talked me into buying it for Ma's birthday, hosted at the restaurant Mic worked. Mic had 'curated' the meal, his word, which I think means 'planned and prepped'. But he enjoyed eating it with us. Best of both worlds. The train ride, over four hours north, took me through the leafy state of Connecticut and up to Massachusetts. I'd left early, at six o'clock, so I'd be eyeballing O'Neil before lunch. While I had the latest copy of *Time* on my lap, the numbness from my arm seemed to spread through to my whole body. I stared out the window and saw nothing.

The central business district of Boston is known for its old buildings of grandeur, but it has some new shiny tall ones as well. Much to O'Neil's delight, no doubt. I found his office in one of those tall and shiny buildings. It was easy enough. The address was listed on his business website, and Google Maps took me straight to it. The front entrance had a large glass door rather than the automated sliding variety. I took hold of the large handle with my good hand, soon discovering that the door was indeed automated. It swung me purposefully inside the expansive foyer, almost dislocating my elbow. The glass theme continued inside, along with generous slabs of black marble. There were two dark grey leather couches with chrome legs placed in an alcove to my left, looking like the plastic wrapping had just come off them. I resisted the urge to curl up on one, nursing both injured arms. Glancing around the reflective surfaces, no security counter was apparent. Resisting temptation, I pressed on in search of O'Neil. My arms throbbed as I hunted for a building directory, eventually spotting it hidden behind a square column of marble. O'Neil's company, Kinsale Developments Pty Ltd on level ten. Riding up in an elevator of smoked mirrors, the doors soon opened to a large photograph of rocks by the ocean, hanging on an off-white wall. With jaw set, I ignored the pain of my arms and walked with a stride across the beige marble flooring (on better days I would have taken my shoes of and slid), leading to the company's reception and foyer. A well-groomed woman of about thirty sat behind a desk that reminded me of sports commentary shows on television. She even had the headset. I felt like jumping in behind there and telling her all about Robert William's torn meniscus in his left knee that may put him out for the season. Instead, I behaved like the perfect gentlemen and asked after O'Neil. Expressionless, she asked, 'Do you have an appointment, sir?'

'No,' I replied with the light chuckle I had rehearsed the day before. 'I'm family. Just in town for the day, thought I could lure the old guy out for a beverage.'

'I'm afraid Mr O'Neil is not in the office. Can I take a message?'

'Is his PA available? Tabitha MacLaine?' Old guard, Tabby

MacLaine. After all the telephone messages, I knew the name backwards.

'I'll just check for you, Mr?'

'Call me Roberto. I'm up from New York. Ms MacLaine will know who I am.' *Should* know who I am. Then again, maybe I'm just one of many pissed sons-in-law-once-removed.

The woman smiled and nodded. While calling through the computer before her, she gestured to the leather seats near the desk. Mustard yellow couches with chrome legs, similar to the grey ones in the building entrance foyer. I sat down on one of them, imagining the reflection off the leather would make anyone jaundiced. I held my elbows. Everything ached. I strained to hear what sweet nothings were being murmured into her little microphone. All I heard was 'Mr Roberto' then 'Tabitha will be out in a minute.' She was talking to me. With headsets, it's always hard to tell. I nodded, and my knees snapped into a vertical position. After five minutes of standing to attention, a woman in a navy pinstriped suit with bouncing red hair breezed out from behind the reception wall.

'Mr Roberto,' she held out her hand in greeting. 'I'm Tabitha MacLaine.'

'Please, call me Roberto.' What I wanted to say was: *Please call me Roberto if you can't remember my last name from all the emails and phone calls. 'Mr Roberto' is ludicrous.* I always assumed that women called Tabitha were cute. Even though the woman had been a thorn in my side for weeks, I had hoped that she had a button nose at least. Not this one. She was attractive but in an elegant, handsome way. And had corporate loyalty written all over her.

'Unfortunately, Mr O'Neil is currently away on business. I'm sure he would be sad to hear he missed you.'

'Devastated,' I replied, the light chuckle reappearing, this time with a hint of hysteria.

Tabby stiffened but kept her poise. 'Can I take a message for you?'

'I just wanted to know why he stole my forty percent of the Houston Street project. I've racked my brains over it and, well, just looking at the foyer here, I can see how hard-pressed for cash you guys are. It must be a struggle living hand to mouth like this, Tab. How do you manage?'

'I can see that you are upset, Mr Roberto-'

'No, upset is when I throw hot oil on myself,' I said, which put her on pause for a moment.

'I'm sure there's been a misunderstanding,' she said, rolling over my comment. 'I will have Mr O'Neil contact you as soon as possible to explain to you the process.'

'Explain to me the process of theft?' I was yelling now.

'Terrence?' the receptionist said to her microphone. 'Yes, we might need you.'

'I can't help you,' Tabitha replied with the firm tone of a well-versed bureaucrat. 'But I will pass on your message.'

'As you have every day I've emailed? Every time I've called?'

'Yes,' she said, almost with defiance. Tabitha would make an excellent German Shepherd. 'Do have a safe trip back to New York, Mr Roberto,' she said, turning to walk back behind the reception wall barricade.

'I'm not going. For all I know, O'Neil is just behind that wall there.' I moved fast towards the doorway, intending to overtake Tabitha and cross enemy lines. But the PA was sure on her Manolo Blahniks and managed to block my path, as did the receptionist. It's extraordinary how responsive people can be when it suits them. I tried struggling past, but a well-built security officer (the Cloisters could have used him) appeared from behind and grabbed my burnt wrist with a grip that could mince a raw potato. I cried out in pain and retreated to the couch.

'I'll stay here until O'Neil decides to come out,' I snarled, holding my arm.

'As already explained,' Tabitha said, 'Mr O'Neil is not here.'

'I'll just sit here anyway,' I replied, shifting my focus onto the security guard. I knew what was coming, but I was beyond reason. 'These couches are so comfortable.'

'I'm afraid that's not possible,' Tabitha said. 'If you persist, Terence here will have to escort you out of the building.'

I tested the theory and found myself back on the Amtrak in less than half an hour. Kinsale Developments, a place where everyone knows your name - and where you live. I needed someone in my corner, someone who got angrier more effectively than I did. Put simply, I needed a lawyer. On the train, I searched my phone for a contract law specialist. I looked for someone who wasn't going to cost the earth using the keywords 'cost-effective' and 'small company'. I found three names in the New York City area. Back in Manhattan, emerging out of Central Station, I left messages with all of them. I then went for a walk to clear my head. Artie had called several times, but I had nothing to say just yet. Avoiding the office completely, I'd emailed feel-good messages like 'I'm on it, boss', 'Think I've got a juicy one'. The hard edge was yet to come. Whatever that was.

It was five o'clock by the time I made it to the bar where Pete and I used to chew the fat. It was the time of day when the late sun shone directly through the windows, making it harder to see. Or was stress now affecting my eyesight? With my sunglasses on, I could still barely make out the place as I picked my way around the tables. The glow of the tv screen behind the bar helped the deeper I went. The Yankees were pitching, and the score was looking promising. I made my way to my regular seat at the bar, which was out of the glare of the sunlight. Removing my sunglasses, Kahlil had already placed a Corona down, top off. I sent him a smile and felt myself begin to unwind. The foam on the beer sat at a happy minimum. I wanted to marry the place.

The longer I sat on the stool, the more my eyes adjusted, and I could make out what was around me. The wood panelling, the framed sports photographs, an old guy sitting five seats away and two middle-aged men sat at a table discussing horse racing tips. Kahlil asked how I was. I said 'Okay'. I asked how he was. He said 'Okay.' He looked at my bandaged hand, asked if it was okay. I said yes, adding 'Cooking oil'. Then he left me alone with my golden ale and thoughts of Gerry.

Yes, Gerry still came to mind. I kept her fixed in the realm of fantasy. She had become a mental escape hatch from the stink of the shit around me. Considering current circumstances, to call her now would be like hitting a singles bar after being diagnosed with testicular cancer. It wouldn't be fair to anyone. I didn't even know if she was single. She could be married with kids for all I knew. She could be the type not to wear a ring, or not to wear a ring while gardening, or not to get married at all. Whatever her reality, it seemed I'd never have the balls anyway.

Chapter Five

The next day was Friday. Gab's birthday. I had posted her present earlier in the week. A deluxe painting set with a card sincerely apologising for my absence and a request for something to decorate my office partition wall. If the communication was going to see me in jail, I didn't care.

Two out of the three lawyers called back that day. More accurately, their PAs did. I gave as much information as I could over the phone to get an idea of what the process might cost me. If I got my money back, it would be worth it. If I didn't, I'd be bankrupt. The fees were about the same. But both told me not to get ahead of myself. Just to come in for a preliminary meeting and work out best steps from there. I chose one by tossing a coin–heads to win–and made an appointment with Singer & Dalton. There had just been a cancellation for Monday morning. I could be slipped in. The appointment would be brief, but it was a start. I was advised to gather all documentation, namely the emails and any notes I might have made in response to phone conversations. I did this and went one step further, looking up O'Neil's company website again. They liked touting themselves so, in a matter of seconds, I possessed a comprehensive list of Kinsale's developments to date. The Houston brownstone, still in progress, wasn't one of them. Thinking of the Philadelphia court case that had frozen O'Neil's finances earlier, I checked the court notes. After multiple searches, I found O'Neil had allegedly taken some construction shortcuts and an alleged attempted bribe was made with a Philadelphia council evaluator. But evidence was scant. The project manager was penalised, but O'Neil's hands came out clean. Undeterred, I made a call to Jim, a buddy of mine at the City Council. Since I'd done the council a ton of favours in the past, giving essentially free publicity for events, Jim and I got along fine. I was after information about O'Neil's projects in New York. Namely, who at the Council approved his plans and site inspections. If it was the same person, I had a shot at something. Maybe.

Artie called again, leaving a message of 'What the fuck is going on? Where the fuck are you?' I emailed back that I was working from home, not to worry and to have a nice weekend. If Artie had weekends, that is. I then made my way to Ma's for dinner, picking up some Thai on the way as promised.

Looking at my bandaged arm, she asked, 'You okay?'

I said 'Yep' and began dishing out the panang curry.

Ma had been at Gab's party that afternoon. As planned, the kids and parents had met at the zoo after school to celebrate. I didn't feel like asking but she gave me the rundown of attendees, quality of gifts, food, and the weather pattern during the afternoon, with intermittent chides on my non-appearance.

'How could you not be there?' she asked, slamming the palm of her hand on the kitchen counter. 'What could be more important?'

'Was Mic there?'

She shook her head like I was an idiot. 'He work.'

'So do I, Ma. Things are changing at the magazine.' She looked at me with suspicion, unconvinced. But nothing more was said on the matter. We bypassed the bamboo chopsticks and shovelled the food into our mouths with forks in front of the television. Tonight was a forensic drama which somehow held my attention. During a commercial break, I caught my mother looking at me. She then patted my knee, almost knocking my plate to the floor.

I hadn't mentioned the development to Ma. Not once. I knew she would worry even when it was all looking great. But that night I had to ask a question, and I asked it in Italian. 'What do you really think about Mic, Ma?'

'Weak' she replied in English.

'And Mr O'Neil, Mic's dad?'

'Fascist, like Mussolini. But worse.'

She was concise. I gave her that.

'How do you know? How can you be so sure?' She shrugged her shoulders as she turned back to the television. I mumbled to myself in English, 'It makes me wonder what you think about me.'

'As beautiful as a spring day.' Though she replied in Italian, that she understood me indicated her English was improving. Maybe television had a purpose after all. I laughed at the reply. As a mother, she had an obligation to be biased. Her expression then altered to sadness, 'And you are trusting.'

I put my arm around her and gave her a squeeze. 'You're my only family, Ma.'

She shook her head. 'Don't you worry. Sophia's just gone away for a while. She'll be back.' Just when I was going to ask her what she meant, what she knew, stations were switched by remote. On the screen was Raymond's father again, and Ma was immediately hooked. There would be no talking with her now. I put my empty plate on the floor and sat back, guessing how the other show was going to end.

The weekend was long, every minute was like an hour that had put on weight. Cabin fever struck early in the apartment. On

Saturday afternoon, I grabbed my keys and wallet, and caught the Circle Line ferry to putt around Manhattan Island with the rest of the sightseers. It was a tourist and school kid activity. A fully-grown New Yorker would never do this. Nor would he climb the Statue of Liberty, which I also did. When looking for some perspective, getting out on the perimeter sometimes helps, as does getting some height. But being continuously wind- swept and jostled, however, made this goal almost impossible. For the most part, I got caught up and was transported by people in anoraks. There was the odd moment when I saw my town from a distance, and it looked like a place I was just visiting. The afternoon confirmed what I always knew. To experience New York City, you must be in it. Just looking didn't cut it.

On Monday, I waited in the Singer & Dalton's reception area for over half an hour. It was nothing like Kinsale's. For a start, they had opted for vinyl flooring over marble. Behind the cheap timber veneer reception desk sat a young guy called Craig. He wasn't graced with a sports desk headset, just a standard phone with a handful of lines. Behind Craig was a large, framed photo of the Chrysler Building, which we weren't in, but it made me wish we were. A couple of calls came through as I sat opposite in one of a row of blue plastic chairs. The rest were empty. I had plenty of time to study Craig, not that I wanted to. His nervous disposition was enhanced by the fluorescent lighting and red acne contrasting with his pale skin. The cheap white shirt he chose to wear that morning wasn't doing him any favours. I kept scrolling news feeds on my phone to distract myself.

According to my watch, the clock on my phone and the one on the wall near Craig all said my brief legal appointment allocation had come and gone, but eventually I was introduced to Morris Dalton. He was just under six-foot, short back and sides with a lanky figure. I was hoping for a ball-breaker, a hungry one. Instead, I could imagine Dalton helping his wife to win best marmalade at the country fair. He led me into his office.

The interior was a notch up from reception but not by much. Rather than the dark wood panelling and green glass lamp shades I had come to expect from movies on fighting for justice, there was a veneer desk laden with piles of paper, folders on the verge of sliding off the edge, and two medium-sized computer screens side-by-side. The room was lined with mis-matching veneer bookshelves and grey filing cabinets. The window looked out on more unassuming buildings like this one. Some sun was coming in and hitting the desk, which eased my nerves a tad. Morris Dalton liked to swivel in his modest office chair, which I did my best to ignore. While swivelling he flipped through my printed-out emails, downloaded web notes and copied signed documents. The paperless office was clearly an ambition for the long-term. Still, I was glad Morris appeared to be across the content, demonstrated by his re-cap of the disaster that was my life. We were both on the same page.

'No joint venture contract,' he commented.

'Only verbally.'

'Okay,' he swivelled, 'First up, let's try and spook them.' It was a little Walt Disney for my taste, so I was about to suggest, 'How about scaring the crap out of them instead?' but he intercepted. 'We want to get their attention and find a resolve through a process of discussion. Organised mediation if we must. Going to court is a last measure.' I nodded, disappointed, and moved position in my non-swivel chair. I was hoping to serve subpoenas. I've always liked the word 'subpoena', almost as much as the phrase 'You have the right to an attorney'.

Dalton continued, 'I will organise a caveat on the property with the Land Titles Office.'

'A caveat?'

'It will prevent them from selling any aspect of the property.'

'Does it stop the renovations?'

'No, that can continue. It's probably a good idea to email Mr O'Neil and…' he paused, looking at his notes for the name of the other party, which was Mic, '…Mr O'Neil, warning them that this will happen tomorrow. You will also be best to write a letter to both parties. Title all correspondence 'Without Prejudice'.'

'Why?'

'It means they can't use the contents of the letter in court,' he explained and moved on. 'The letter is to outline what has happened to date as you see it and to reinforce information pertaining to the caveat. The letter also announces a final opportunity for them to either create a joint venture agreement containing what had already been agreed to verbally earlier or pay out your share with interest. If neither option is taken, then proceedings will commence within the next three months, initiated by this firm.'

'Proceedings?' By this stage, I was taking notes, grateful for my journalistic shorthand.

Dalton nodded, 'Yes. Give a deadline of a week for a response, putting the date in bold. Do not, and I repeat, do not use emotional language in this letter. Be cool, calm and professional. After you have drafted it, email it to me. Once we are both happy with it, my office will then express deliver it to both parties. We will make sure they have to sign for it personally.'

'I have a problem,' I said, lifting my pen for attention. 'Mic's put a restraining order on me.'

'Mic? Oh, the son, Michael,' Dalton checked back on his records. 'Criminal or Family Court?'

'Family.'

'Well, that's good,' he laughed and swivelled. 'You'd have charges against you already if it was criminal.'

After releasing a laugh of my own, hollow with serrated edges, I said, 'Apparently, I'm not allowed to correspond with him, or send messages to him through someone else.'

'When do you have your hearing?'

'In about a month.'

'Okay, so that means we can't touch Mic for now. But Grand Daddy-o is still in the game. He seems to be the ringleader, anyway. Mr O'Neil doesn't have a restraining order against you too, does he?'

'No, not yet,' I said, thinking of my Boston visit.

'Good. Are you clear that you are to draft the letter outlining the facts as you see them and email it to me? But before doing that, simply email the father, warning him of the caveat and to expect a letter. Head your correspondence: "Without Prejudice". That's all. Keep it brief, clear and without emotion. It helps build the suspense.'

Helps build the suspense? To Dalton, this may as well have been a fictional story. A plot, a climax with a fee at the end.

'What if this gets to court? What are my chances?'

'None of the previous cases Mr O'Neil senior has been involved in will be admissible. While the emails indicate your participation in the Houston Street project, the agreement remains unsigned. The property is in his company's name. That's also unfortunate. However, there is the transfer of funds from your account. Plus, O'Neil will look bad if they lie in court, which they are bound to do to some extent. There is a case for you, a good one. But it's not watertight.'

'There's a chance I might not win?'

'Yes.'

Suddenly, the Walt Disney approach didn't look like such a bad idea after all. Leaving with my list of things to do, I did my best to think positive. But it was hard to disregard the sense of shame that inevitably settles when people start ghosting you.

I once dated a woman called Delta, who was very in touch with her feelings. She had therapy once a week and all sorts of groups in which to discuss and share experiences. They would even gather at my place sometimes, having more space in my lounge area than Delta's bedsit in the Village. The members looked normal except for the slightly widened eyes. Naturally, my girlfriend tried to lure me in. But I resisted, knowing that level of analysis would unravel my sanity like those little pull-string pop-out streamers. The thing that always had me diving for the television, the bar or the office was when Delta suggested I should write about what's bothering me.

'I'm a journalist,' I grunted. 'I write for a living. I don't want to do it in my spare time, too.'

But that day, after the meeting with my lawyer, it seemed possible the woman had a point. Back home, I sat down and wrote. After emailing the warning to O'Neil and the letter to Dalton for editing, I let loose on a blank page of my laptop. It wasn't like the diary of some teenage girl, but I allowed more emotion than I usually do for work.

After half an hour of key tapping, the phone rang. Expecting it to be Artie, I steeled myself before picking up. But it was Jim, my buddy at the City Council. His name was actually James Brown. Being of African heritage, short, thin, with a big smile, he never heard the end of it. The name was Jim instead.

'Hey, Roberto. I've got your answer on this O'Neil guy and his past developments in New York. Busy, isn't he?'

'Developers usually are, I guess,' I replied. 'You've found out who in Council has approved his plans?

'And site inspections, yeah,' he said. 'As you thought, it's all been the same person, George Dodt, which is unusual. We've got policies preventing that sort of thing. Plus, people move around so much, which it makes it hard to have that kind of continuity anyway.'

'George Dodt,' I said, thinking *he even sounds like a public servant.* 'Why has this happened? George doing all the paperwork every time?'

'A friend like George could speed up the approvals, I guess. It's the old saying, time is money.'

'The mantra of our generation,' I agreed. 'In Philadelphia, O'Neil was suspected of bribing a council valuer.'

'To do a half-arsed job and get away with it?'

'That was it exactly. Do you think O'Neil may have done the same in New York?'

My friend whistled, thankfully away from the phone. 'It would be hard to pull off. Surely someone would smell something fishy once the complaints came in.'

'But that would take a while. Maybe long enough to get the dough you need for an early retirement.'

'I wonder if George is still around…'

'Could you find out for me, Jim? In the meantime, I'll check out the body corporates of the buildings, see if they have anything to tell me about shoddy work.'

'I'll do my best from this end. A lot of complaints go through the council but are fast-tracked to the insurance company to settle,' Jim explained. 'The next conversation we both have is face-to-face. In cognito. I'll give you another call, or a carrier pigeon with a note around its neck.'

'How about a woman in a black hat?'

'I'll do my best.'

'Thanks, Jim.'

I did my share of the sniffing. Some body corporates were happy to oblige. Others were cloak and dagger. That's the way with people and the media. It's all or nothing - an opportunity to complain or get a bit of fame, or complete fear of exposure, any exposure. I even tried talking to the foreman on the Houston site, but he had learnt to staple his lips, probably getting a bonus from O'Neil for doing so. I didn't know if the work was good or bad by just looking at it, so I left.

The next day, Dalton approved my letter, so that was now being sent out. O'Neil hadn't responded to my email. Nothing new there. Jim got back to me later that day, and we met at a basement café, the sort of place where wholemeal pancakes and soup abound. It had been Jim's choice. I ordered a non-soy coffee, while Jim had a freshly-squeezed beetroot and celery juice, with a touch of ginger. It looked as bad as it sounded.

'Your hand okay?' he asked. The plastic had been removed, giving it air to heal. I had some scabs forming. It was progress.

'Much better, thanks.'

The place was pretty quiet, but we settled at a corner table anyway. 'George left a few months ago,' Jim started. 'He was about sixty years old. The fool had his eye on a young administrative officer. Told her about his place in the Hamptons and then another at Martha's Vineyard, trying to lure her up to either for a weekend. Showed her pictures, as if it would help. He had been a menace to her for months. She'd been thinking of submitting a sexual abuse statement, but his early retirement was announced just in time. The woman despised George with a passion. She was happy to tell me the story, her eyes rolling constantly like a horse in pain.'

'The pictures were impressive?' I asked, taking a sip of my coffee. The taste was terrible. I poured in another sachet of sugar.

'Not to her. But, yes, they were large, expensive properties. I looked him up, and they are in George's name, valued at about 1.5 mill apiece.'

'He must've had one hell of a retirement party.' I tasted the coffee again, realising nothing was going to save it.

'If he did, I wasn't invited. Sure would have liked to have been there, knowing what I know now.'

'Ah, hindsight,' I said staring at the wall behind him for a moment. Hindsight is easy, a walk in the park. You can see all the signs you hadn't spotted before. Hindsight has a habit of pointing the finger and saying, 'Told you so, saucepan head.' I moved on. 'I imagine these retirement oases are more than what modest council wages can bear.'

'Just a tad, or I'm missing out on some serious action,' Jim said, sipping his pinky-brown swill. He seemed quite happy with it. 'You asked about insurance. A serious number of claims have come through from O'Neil's developments, post-sale. I was surprised that the insurance company hadn't placed their own protest. I called one of the managers there. Apparently, George already had his fingers slapped rather badly just before the retirement date.'

'He knew he was in hot water, and it was time to jump out.'

'George's assistant, Tom Lewis, worked closely with George for over a year. Tom assumed his position and was lined up to approve the Houston project.'

'Ah, the passing down of wisdom.'

'Quite possibly, but not yet verified.'

I took down the name and number of the insurance contact and the administrative officer, just in case. I couldn't afford to pay Jim for his efforts, and he was insulted that I should mention such a thing. The next day, he'll find tickets on his desk. Good seats for the next two Nix games. Not on the court but close enough.

Thanking Jim, I threw my money for the drinks on the table and made my way home.

Chapter Six

At the end of the week, Dalton reported the O'Neils were standing firm, prepared to go to court if need be. I advised Dalton to pause before proceeding. He queried my motive, but all I could say was that it was a family matter.

A little package arrived at Mr O'Neil's home on the Saturday morning, special delivery. It was the sort of package that got a response.

'What do you want, kid?' His tone had shifted from the usual weary and condescending to terse and impatient.

'A meeting at the Metropolitan Museum on Sunday morning.'

'Sunday morning is church.'

'Church?' I almost gagged on my own breath when he said it. 'Mid-afternoon then.' Then he would drive down from Boston. We agreed to meet in the Asian artefacts section. Just O'Neil and me, Mic knew none of this. Asia was quieter than the rest of the place and had a bench where we could sit. I was early. A gold bodhisattva with twelve arms was perched in a case in front of me. All the hands and arms were in excellent condition.

O'Neil came empty-handed. My jaw clenched in fury.

'We have to go back down, Roberto. They wouldn't let me bring the bag in. Security.'

Best laid plans. We walked together back down to the entrance. I held the brown leather bag for him like a platter while he checked the contents, back to the wall. The foyer was crammed with the Sunday crowd, worshippers of art.

'It looks like it's all still there,' he nodded. 'But we need to go somewhere…'

'More discrete,' I said loudly, hoping to create an echo around the marble surfaces. O'Neil snapped the case and headed for the exit. We wandered out onto Fifth Avenue, then meandered into Central Park. The air was getting cooler, keeping the public mostly to homeless and hired dog walkers. O'Neil seemed unsatisfied with the environment. I didn't understand why we couldn't just go to my apartment. But it didn't seem to be the way business was done, too cottage industry maybe.

'I know somewhere that's quiet and dimly-lit,' I volunteered. 'It's just across the park.'

'How far, walking distance?'

I was tempted to suggest a brisk jog, test his ticker, but instead hailed a horse and carriage stationed nearby.

'You're kidding?' O'Neil said as I held out my good hand from the carriage.

'Not the romantic type, are you, sir?' He took my hand and climbed on anyway. The mare trotted off towards Central Park West.

Playing host on behalf of the city, I pointed out the Park's Belvedere Castle and Turtle Pond. I was delighted to indicate the Delacorte Theatre up ahead, where Shakespeare's plays were performed for free during the summer. O'Neil didn't appear to be one for sights. He was in development after all, a specialist in what wasn't there yet. After only just stretching my arm around O'Neil's shoulders, the horse pulled up to our stop.

I emphatically insisted on paying, although O'Neil didn't move to offer, and gave the horseman a generous tip. Alighting from the carriage, we wandered across the road and paid an entry fee for the Hayden Planetarium. The bag was permitted. Or, in other words, no one stopped us. We found some seats in a quiet back corner near Pluto, which had its own irony. Turned out Pluto wasn't what we thought it was. In 2006 it had been downgraded from planet to dwarf planet. Something about gravitational dominance in the neighbourhood. I counted the money by the light of the sun emitted from the other end of the room. The cash was bound in hundreds and my hand still ached, so the process was longer than what we both liked.

There weren't many people at the Plantarium that afternoon. Those who were there paid most attention to the sun, Saturn or Earth. The big, the beautiful and the personally relevant. Pluto was too small and far away to be of much interest. Except for little Henry who orbited us several times until his mother called for him from Mars.

'Your hand looks bad,' O'Neil commented when I finished.

'It's getting better,' I said, untouched.

'You would have noticed there's a bonus in there. A quite substantial bonus.'

'I noticed,' I said. 'I deserve it.'

'Anyway, that's it then?'

'That's it,' I said.

'You won't be slipping a word to the fellas at the station?'

'The police station?'

He rolled his eyes, 'Yes, the police station. I have your word?'

'You have my word.'

My word, with nothing in writing. I was secretly pleased with the bonus and with the bag that looked Italian, genuine leather. After leaving the galaxy and arriving home, I gave the case closer inspection. The bag was a rip-off, synthetic. The money was all there, still real greenbacks, and that's what counted.

I didn't go to the police, as promised. I went to Artie instead. The article on O'Neil appeared in a fortnight, double spread full colour, with instalments to appear in following issues. The by-line was passed to two young jocks on the team, my request. I remained anonymous. O'Neil would have put two and two together. He was furious but by that stage he had police all over him like a rash. My hunch was that O'Neil, while being a heavy hitter, was not one for hit men. He was a white-collar criminal who operated through financial persuasion and clever paper work, even when angry. I hoped my hunch was right. As backup, I spent as much time in crowds as possible the following weeks.

Magazine sales went through the roof. The public seemed to have a special hatred reserved for shonky developers, particularly in their neck of the woods. Bad building was one thing. A multitude of stories describing unhealthy living from damp, un-vermin proofed buildings created sympathy from readers. Unsafe foundations made the future shaky for all. Personal stories of near-death experiences hit the home run. There were a nice handful of those, usually to do with electrics, all pointing the finger to one company. Kinsale Pty Ltd.

The silent body corporates changed their tune once they knew they were on safe ground. The insurance company got on board. Television hooked up the story and ran with it. Independent reports on council procedure were in flight. Kinsale was in serious trouble. And previously paid-off foremen and builders were getting their fair share of the heat. George Dodt's relaxing retirement finished early as his assistant took advantage of the spotlight. The Philadelphia case reopened on new evidence. Other owners of Kinsale developments outside of New York caught on. O'Neil became a national story.

'I didn't know you had it in you,' Artie said, slapping me on the back. 'I look forward to more of the same.'

'To be honest, Artie, I don't think I do have it in me.'

'Okay,' Artie sighed. 'You've saved your bacon for a year. You want to continue as before.'

'No.'

'No?'

'I also want a column in sports.'

'Sports?'

'I know Griff's is leaving.' Griffin was in sports. His wife, the breadwinner of his household, had been transferred to Chicago. Hang around the coffee pot enough, you get the important news. 'You know you've got the space.'

'Okay,' Artie agreed. 'Three months trial, then a review.'

'Six months on my original income, plus twenty percent for sports. Not including expenses. Then a review in six months for a pay rise.'

'You're a cocky bastard all of a sudden,' Artie said, leaning back in his chair, considering his options. Eventually, he said, 'Ah, what the hell.'

The temporary restraining order was removed before the hearing. Soph did her best to make amends, explaining she was told 'versions of the truth' from Mic and his father. I didn't listen much but heard the restaurant dream had been suspended. She and Mic were still together but heavy in marriage guidance counselling. A day will come when I'll be able to eat with them again, but I have trouble imagining it.

I took the girls to the Cloisters on Family Day. Being in the penalty box, Soph and Mic were not invited. Instead, Gerry came with us. It was an unusual first date but appropriate, considering how we met. We wandered through the museum but were drawn outside when the sun came out after an overcast morning. The girls ran around the old Cloister columns while Gerry and I looked out over the courtyard gardens nearby. The herbs and trees, planted by the Harlem community group exactly as done before, were doing well. Gerry gave an entertaining tour, explaining what embarrassing medical problems could be remedied with which plants. She then spoke a little more generally and a little more seriously about gardens, the ones before us and some from others she had been a part of in her earlier years. It turned out her real love was for trees, which was why she liked Central Park so much.

The courtyard got me thinking about the money returned, the bonus and what should be done with it all. I was no Rockefeller, but the thought of donating at least a good portion to a cause was a possibility, maybe one involving a community garden where the community was having a hard time coming up for air. I kept these thoughts to myself as we wandered further, keeping an eye on the girls. Other families were mingling, squatting, and smelling the flowers and herbs. We were standing in the Unicorn Garden, where we first met. I could see the similarities between the Unicorn tapestries inside and the garden outside. An impressive effort had been made to maintain the past, and associated fantasies.

The kids were being rounded up by a guide for a story, then to make stained glass windows out of cellophane. It was much darker inside. Walking around the spot lit exhibits it seemed that turning imagination into reality was what made life truly exceptional. Particularly when Gerry took her rough hand into mine in front of a sixteenth century Virgin Mary. By then my wounds had almost healed. And I'll tell you one thing, it felt better than good.

BOOK CLUB QUESTIONS

1. In *Whole & Torn* (Story1), how important was it that Jessica was in a wheelchair for the story? In your opinion, what were Jessica's strengths? How well is the art sector embracing the challenge of environmental sustainability? Why is the cookie for this story called Sprinkle Cookie?

2. In *Call Waiting* (Story 2), was Fleur's aspiration for a tree change idealistic? Was her friend Pete's aspiration to 'make it in New York' idealistic? Have you ever wanted to leave everything for somewhere else completely different? Did you act on the impulse? If so, was it harder than you imagined? Has anyone identified a talent in you that you didn't see in yourself? Why is the cookie for this story called Organic Oatmeal Cookie?

3. In *The Conditional Gift* (Story 3), how much did you feel what Graham was going through in terms of physical challenges? Do you have, or have you had, a health condition that has made doing the simplest things difficult? Do you think those trying to help Graham were successful? How might they have been more helpful? How did you feel at the end of the story? Why do you think the author finished it that way? Why is the cookie for this story called Egg-Free Sugar Cookie?

4. While reading *A Girls' Guide to Fire* (Story 4), did you think that Carla should leave Howard? If so, after finishing

the story, was your mind changed? Thinking about both Carla and Howard, what does the story say about career ambition? What do you think were the main areas of stress for Carla's and Howard's relationship? Do you think the stresses explained their behaviour towards each other? How common are these areas of stress in couple relationships you know? Why is the cookie for this story called Burnt Butter & Toffee Cookie?

5.   In *The Hidden People* (Story 5), "This is my time" was mentioned in different ways. What does the story say about the meaning behind this phrase? The story explains how differently business was conducted once when relationships were more personal. What were the main benefits of this? Do you think doing business with those we don't know well can alter our sense of accountability? How does the story address mental health in family and in business? Why is the cookie for this story called Cream-Filled Chocolate Cookie?

6.   In *Confessions of the Body* (Story 6), the main character has a chronic health condition. How important was it to have Gus as a health advocate to get her through her challenges? How would she have managed without him? How does the experience transform both of them? How important were Gus' homemade trophies and why? Why is the cookie for this story called Drop Cookie?

7.   How does the story *Taxi Outlaw* (Story 7) address the problem of making early assumptions about people?

What does the story say about taking risks for one's art? What does the main character learn about sound in nature? Why is the cookie for this story called Chocolate Crackle Cookie?

8. What does the story *Joint Venture* (Story 8) say about doing business with family members? Should Roberto have chosen not to help Mic because he is family? How does The Cloisters mirror Roberto's feelings of vulnerability? Did you guess how the story was going to end? How did the family betrayal help Roberto transform himself? Why is the cookie for this story called Big Donut Cookie?

9. Why do you think this collection of stories is called *Cookie Jar?*

10. Which story did you like the most and why?

11. Which story did you like the least and why?

12. Do you prefer short stories to novels? Why/why not?

ENJOYED COOKIE JAR?

PLEASE WRITE A REVIEW!

Amazon, Goodreads, wherever you can. It really helps,
particularly if it's positive.

SUBSCRIBE

Subscribe to Megan's somewhat sporadic blog
(you won't be bombarded):
https://meganhillsbooks.com/free-story

FOLLOW AND CHAT

Follow and chat with Megan on Facebook and Instagram
@MeganHillsBooks

READ MEGAN'S NOVEL!

Have a taste…..

PAVLOVA RISING

CHAPTER 1

I raised my partially frozen fist to the door, ready to knock. Then I heard, 'Fuck.' The expletive from the other side could have only come from the very depths of despair. I pressed my ear to the timber, but no other sounds followed. After knocking firmly, I waited. Nothing. Taking a deep breath, I grabbed hold of the icy brass doorknob, tightened my grip on my messenger bag and headed in. The first thing that hit me was the heat. Perry was English, I reminded myself. The man understands interior temperature control. Australians are useless at this.

At this point, Perry should be doing one of three things: sitting behind the desk, standing at one of bookshelves that lined three of the walls, or gazing out the single window which revealed an embarrassing mishmash of architecture inflicted on university campus over the last hundred years, and the city of Sydney beyond. But I couldn't see him. Anywhere.

'Dr Perry?'

Like most, I'd first heard about Perry from his book Hot Culture – Art Theft in the Twentieth Century. With large glossy colour images on even larger amounts of white space, the book had made criminal activity look like a new interior design approach. Sales had rocketed internationally. Perry was launched out of academia and onto people's coffee tables. The fine art expert had become an unlikely celebrity. His photo was everywhere, depicting a dashing dark-haired intellectual wearing a black t-shirt under black leather jacket. Perry's blue eyes were far from angelic. His mouth had the grin of someone who had nabbed the last biscuit from the tin. Perry was forty-four years old. A tidy number, much like my own twenty-two years. Strong and perfectly balanced, I thought. Seeing the man now, other words came to me. A large, pink, sweaty face had risen from behind the desk. His crop of greying brown hair looked like a playful parent had just ruffled it. Weight gain had occurred somewhere between jobs. A lot of weight.

'Anna Lissam?'

'Er, yes,' I nodded.

'My computer has gone completely blank,' Perry said, pushing his dark-rimmed spectacles up the bridge of his bulbous nose. Can a nose put on weight? 'Blank for no reason at all,' he added.

It appeared the new faculty head had been investigating a computer cable, following its lead in the hope of a rainbow. I worked my way carefully around the desk to take a closer look. The screen was indeed at its blackest. Pressing control+alt+delete achieved nothing.

'You need to restart,' I said.

'Bugger,' Perry groaned, working his way back onto his feet.

That was when I first noticed the stain on his light blue shirt, an unfortunate brown smudge in the shape of Africa. Somalia and Mauritania peered out from either side of his red tie. The tie wasn't wide enough to hide Tasmania, let alone Africa. His corduroy jacket was too tight to be buttoned.

The computer took forever to crank back up. Being on the precipice of technological disaster, it was clear Perry was not in the mood for chitchat. Digging his fingertips deep into his cheeks, his red-tinged eyes watched the computer, waiting for it to return to consciousness. I stole another glance at his shirt. The stain looked more like shoe polish than coffee. Looking down, his brown leather shoes confirmed it, mid-tan. Had he cleaned them with his shirt and then decided to wear it?

The computer beamed back to life. A document titled 'Aboriginal Art Intro (Recovered)' automatically appeared. Nausea stirred in my stomach.

'Thank god,' Perry said. 'Actually, I should thank you. Well done.'

'Excuse me, Dr Perry,' I started, 'is this document yours?'

'Yes, indeedy,' he replied, relaxing back into the leather office chair.

I walked carefully to the other side of the desk, weighing up my next move. 'You were writing about Australian Aboriginal art?' I asked.

'Yes, for the undergrads,' Perry replied. 'Might seem a little ballsy, being a Pom fresh on Australian shores. But believe me, Lissam, I know a thing or two about Aboriginal daubs.'

That had always been the problem. A thing or two is no way near enough. The man had not yet acclimatised.

Read more when you buy 'Pavlova Rising':
meganhillsbooks.com/buy

About The Author

Cookie Jar is Megan Hills' second book if fiction. In 2022 she published her novel, *Pavlova Rising*. Put nicely, Megan has a peripatetic history. That is, she has had ants in her pants, moving from place to place in search of god knows what. Growing up in Adelaide, South Australia, she moved to Melbourne, then New York, then Sydney, then the seaside town of Portsea, then outside the inland town of Lismore. In some of these places she worked in the rough and tumble world of private art galleries. In Sydney she also worked at an art magazine publishing house as a production manager and graphic designer, which led to a marketing role at a craft and design association in Brisbane. When she moved to Darwin, Megan worked as a cultural enterprise manager for a First Nations organisation and swam occasionally in crocodile infested waters. Moving to the safer paddling spot of Newcastle, Megan now runs her own creative and cultural consultancy, The Creative Ingredient. She works with artists and First Nations knowledge holders any chance she gets.

Author's Thanks

Big hugs to my friends who generously volunteered to read this book in its various awkward incarnations and gave it to me straight, particularly Jeff Shearer, and Kate Gilbert. Pompoms to New York-based Laura Duffy, book cover designer extraordinaire.

You will notice many of the *Cookie Jar* stories have an art focus and some have First Nations characters. Deep gratitude to all the First Nations and non-Indigenous artists I've worked with over the years, who bravely create and share expressions of Connection. We all need reminders we're not alone and that we do better together.

47906CB00003B/871